A quiet English

Trying to escape

teaching position in the village of Market Scarston. But his slow rehabilitation is interrupted when a group of students are apparently attacked by Black Shuck, the legendary demon dog, and Crowley attracts the attention of a secret society dating back to the days of the Roman Empire.

See how it all began for Jake Crowley and Rose Black in this prequel novella, SANCTUM!

PRAISE FOR
DAVID WOOD AND ALAN BAXTER

"Blood Codex is a genuine up all night got to see what happens next thriller that grabs you from the first page and doesn't let go until the last." Steven Savile

"Rip roaring action from start to finish. Wit and humor throughout. Just one question - how soon until the next one? Because I can't wait." Graham Brown

"A page-turning yarn. Indiana Jones better watch his back!"Jeremy Robinson

"A a story that thrills and makes one think beyond the boundaries of mere fiction and enter the world of 'why not'?" David Lynn Golemon,

"A twisty tale of adventure and intrigue that never lets up and never lets go!" Robert Masello

"A fast-paced storyline that holds the reader right from the start,. and a no-nonsense story-telling approach that lets the unfolding action speak for itself." Van Ikin

SANCTUM

A JAKE CROWLEY ADVENTURE

DAVID WOOD
ALAN BAXTER

Adrenaline Press

SANCTUM- A Jake Crowley Adventure
Copyright 2020 by David Wood

Edited by Melissa Bowersock

Published by Adrenaline Press
www.adrenaline.press

Adrenaline Press is an imprint of Gryphonwood Press
www.gryphonwoodpress.com

This is a work of fiction. All characters are products of the
authors' imaginations or are used fictitiously.

ISBN 978-1-950920-12-9

Amber
Justice
Treasure of the Dead
Bloodstorm

Dane Maddock Universe
Berserk
Maug
Elementals
Cavern
Devil's Face
Herald
Brainwash
The Tomb
Shasta

Jade Ihara Adventures
Oracle
Changeling
Exile

Bones Bonebrake Adventures
Primitive
The Book of Bones
Skin and Bones

Myrmidon Files
Destiny
Mystic

Stand-Alone Novels
Into the Woods
Arena of Souls
The Zombie-Driven Life
You Suck
Callsign: Queen

BOOKS BY ALAN BAXTER

Prologue

Oliver Greene walked onto the packed dirt floor of the gloomy underground arena feeling foolish. The air was cool and tickled up goosebumps on his bare arms, legs, and chest. The loincloth he wore fit him well enough, but he still felt like a baby in a ridiculous nappy. The air, pungent with waxy candles, flaming torches on the walls, and some kind of incense, was also close with tension. The flickering torches made shadows dance, adding their own acrid smoke to the wide chamber. All around the raised circumference, fellow teenagers, all clad in togas, began to jeer and shout. Most sounded good-natured enough, but there was an edge to some of the voices, a hint of aggression, the potential for violence. Surely this was all nonsense. He had to assume none of them really took it seriously.

Greene walked down three stone steps into the fighting pit, a circular area some thirty feet in diameter, surrounded by concentric circles of stone terraces where the gathered crowd stood to watch and jeer. A scattering of sand had been spread over the dirt of the floor, rough and cold under his bare feet. In the center of the pit were two straight swords, one across the other like a letter X. Replicas of Roman spatha, straight, double-edged, with a sharp point and a hard, rounded metal pommel at the end of the hilt. Simple, but effective and truly deadly. Greene knew the edges were honed to razor sharpness, he'd handled them before. But never in a fight. They always sparred with dull-edged versions.

Greene stopped and stood right beside the swords, refusing to look at them. He glanced around the crowd of bombastic boys, brow furrowed. His schoolmates were taking this all too seriously. Things were getting out of hand.

And the older members of the club, the alleged adults who ought to know better, had a vicious glee in their eyes that made him weak.

After a moment they fell quiet, a slow reduction of excitement until the chamber rang with silence, swollen with potential. Greene licked his lips, looked around again. No one spoke. Did he really have to go through all the nonsense they had discussed earlier? He wouldn't give them the satisfaction.

A chubby boy stepped forward, eyes dark. "Say the words, Greene."

Oliver sighed, shook his head. "This is stupid."

The shouting and jeering started up again, but the chubby boy held up a hand. "We are in the sanctum," he said, his voice hard and commanding. "You took an oath. Now say the words."

Oliver cleared his throat. "I demand trial by combat." He tried to sound confident, but his voice was hoarse, weak.

"Is there a champion?"

Hushed conversation rippled around the chamber. Oliver's heart raced. Surely no one would actually answer the call. It was all empty ritual, no more than a joke really. Something they acted out up to a point, but there wouldn't really be a fight. A sword fight. With actual sharp blades.

"I will be champion." The voice was low and resonant, instantly recognizable.

Oliver's shoulders sagged. Robert Kray, reputedly a nephew or second cousin or something similar to the notorious Ronnie and Reggie, twin brothers who ruled London in the 50s and 60s with their gang, "The Firm". Robert never let anyone forget his heritage, but Greene wondered if he was simply trading on a shared name. Having said that, Robert was genuinely insane, violent and easily enraged. Perhaps he did have that organized crime blood after all. They had sparred a few times, and Greene knew himself to be evenly matched in skill with Kray, but in a situation like this, Kray's lunacy would surely kick in. He would take this seriously. Kray was also the larger of the two and would press that advantage.

He really is going to try to kill me, Greene thought with a shudder.

Kray removed his toga. He was also clad in one of the ridiculous loincloths underneath. He had obviously planned for the moment. With a wide, predatory grin, he entered the fighting pit.

Each youth picked up one of the replica spatha, the straight sword favored by Roman centurions and gladiators. Greene tried to ignore the trembling in his grip. Kray reached out his right hand, steady as a rock. Drawing a deep breath, steeling himself, Greene shook with him.

Kray leaned in, his voice a harsh whisper. "I'm going to cut your head off."

Greene watched his eyes as Kray leaned back, released the handshake. He didn't look or sound like he was joking. Greene looked around the crowd of boys and men again, their faces alight with elation and expectation. He still couldn't believe everyone was taking this idiocy so seriously, but they clearly were.

Kray tossed the spatha to his right hand and crouched in a ready position. Heart hammering, Greene quickly did the same. If everyone else was treating this as real, he needed to as well.

A voice from the gloom outside the fighting pit said, "Begin!"

Kray launched forward, driving his sword directly for Greene's throat. With a yelp of surprise, Greene danced to the side, sweeping his own blade across to deflect the attack. Kray used the momentum, brought his blade back around, slicing low for Greene's legs. Greene jumped in the air, his feet barely clearing the razor edge. When he landed, he bent his knees, ducked and rolled. His hunch had paid off. Kray grunted in annoyance as he staggered, having expected his strike to find its mark.

Greene tried to take advantage, but as he rose and turned, Kray had already regained his balance and was back on the offensive. The large boy attacked relentlessly, Greene barely managing to hold him off, desperately deflecting the rain of blows. Sweat ran into his eyes, his lungs burned already, the real fight instantly more draining than any amount of sparring. The boys all around them howled and whooped with bloodlust.

Greene made space, sucked in a deep breath. As he moved crabwise around the edge of the pit, Kray attacked again. Greene blocked two hard, fast blows, but the third slipped through and opened a searing wound in Greene's left shoulder. Blood immediately streamed down his arm, began to drip from his fingers, forming scarlet medallions on the dark, sandy floor.

Greene hissed in pain, teeth clenched. "Come on, guys," he shouted over the roaring crowd. "This has gone far enough!"

"You took an oath," a voice called, and then the other boys joined in, chanting it over and over.

"Took an oath! Took an oath!" They began the distinctive stomp-stomp-clap of Queen's "We Will Rock You." It was primal and utterly bizarre.

Stomp-stomp-clap. "Took an oath." *Stomp-stomp-clap.* "Took an oath."

As the chant reverberated through the chamber, Robert Kray grinned and surged forward again, blade flashing left and right.

The pain and the sight of blood made something inside Oliver Greene open up. He thrummed with energy, realized at last, despite his refusals before, that he was genuinely fighting for his life. No longer incredulous, no longer fighting defensively, he met Kray's attack with renewed energy and countered viciously. He marveled at the other boy's look of shock and surprise as he sliced and thrust. Kray misstepped, staggered slightly in a hasty retreat, and Greene opened a cut on his sword arm. Kray hissed, glancing down at the blood that immediately welled into the wound. As he looked up again, he tried a feint, but Greene saw it coming. A quick reversal and then a side swipe and Kray's spatha clattered to the ground, the large boy's face twisted in pain as he shook his stunned hand. He was lucky Greene hadn't chopped it off at the wrist, using the flat of the blade instead in a bit of possibly misplaced mercy. Seeing Kray about to rush him, to turn the sword fight into a wrestling match, Greene quickly turned his weapon sideways and brought the hard pommel across into Kray's temple. The large boy's eyes crossed and he took two rubbery steps, then collapsed onto his knees.

Holding the point of his spatha pointed directly between Kray's eyes, Greene looked up to the chubby boy who had spoken before. "Come on, Arch. It's over."

Arch's face was twisted in something like disgust. He glanced to a young man in the shadows just behind him. The young man nodded and Arch gave a reluctant thumbs-up. Relieved, Oliver dropped his sword and staggered back to slump onto the steps leading into the pit.

Arch folded his arms. "Now you must take the vow of silence, and leave us forever."

Oliver nodded. Right now he'd take any vow if it would get him out of this madhouse.

Oliver ran through the cold night air, dark silhouettes of the forest slipping by in a blur. All he wanted was to get home. After the ridiculous fight, where Kray had done his level best to kill or at least maim him, Greene wanted nothing more than to be far away. He'd taken their stupid vow of silence, agreed to all their ridiculous terms. First thing the next morning he would bully his parents into letting him transfer schools. Maybe even move away, perhaps a long way. There was Uncle Clive in Queensland, after all, who would let him stay. Hell, he'd even be willing to attend an Aussie public school at this point. Finishing his schooling on the other side of the planet seemed like a good idea. Anything to be far away from those nutters.

He slowed his headlong rush and looked around, confused. The trees weren't right. Had he taken a wrong turn in his haste? After everything else this night, it seemed fitting that he would get lost as well. How he wished all this to be behind him.

Something crunched twigs a little way behind. Was someone following him? Greene hurried on, paying a little more attention to his surroundings. The shadows under the trees were pitch, but enough moonlight pierced the branches that he could see his way if he were careful. More sounds behind him. Something had definitely got on his tail. He passed the ruins of an old church and an icy chilled rippled along his veins. His heart raced.

"Black Shuck?" he whispered. Surely not, he didn't deserve such awful luck.

Exhausted from the fight and the subsequent adrenaline comedown, weakened by the pain and blood loss from his shoulder wound, Greene felt lost and adrift. His heart raced and his breath came in ragged gasps. A sob escaped him, and he was close to giving up when he saw the track, realized it was the path to the village he'd been aiming for all along.

"Thank heavens!" he said aloud, vigor returning.

A dark figure stepped out in front of him. "Hello, Oliver."

Greene recognized the face, despite the shadows of a hood. "What are you doing here?"

The dark figure didn't reply. He stepped forward on silent feet. Greene had a moment to see a flash of silver in the moonlight before the large knife drove hard into his chest. Oliver Greene gasped, the pain sudden and total.

And then everything went black. Darkness slowly closed in from the edges of his vision.

1

Market Scarston, Suffolk

Tommy, Chas, Natalie, and Emma scurried across the neatly trimmed grass at the eastern side of Scarsdell Academy and ducked into the shadows of the ancient stone wall. Trying to suppress their panting breaths, making soft clouds in the cool autumn air, they turned as one to look back at the imposing old building. In among the rough-hewn gray blocks of stone that made up its impressive walls, the many windows were mostly dark. They watched, ensuring no further lights came on.

"Okay," Tommy said. "Looks like we got away unseen. Let's go over."

The four teenagers moved along the wall, remaining in its shadow, until they reached a gnarled old oak tree. Its wide and spreading limbs cast even deeper shade over the grass and reached up over the ten-foot-high wall. Tommy wondered how many students over the decades had made their brief escape this way. He patted the old, gnarled trunk in thanks, then made a cradle of his hands and Natalie stepped into it.

"On three, Nat," Tommy said. "One, two, three!" He boosted her up and she caught a low branch and pulled herself onto it.

Chas gave Emma a similar assist, then the two boys, both tall enough to manage on their own, crouched and jumped. They caught the lowest branch and hauled up. All four, grinning and giggling, moved along the branch until they reached the top of the wall. Tommy, Chas, and Emma moved over, sat on the wall, then hopped off, landing with a soft rustle in the leaf litter below.

"I hate this bit!" Natalie said.

Tommy sighed. "You're a gymnast, for goodness sake!"

"But it's the dark that throws me off."

Tommy moved to the wall and reached up. At nearly six feet tall, with long arms, his hands were only a couple of feet from the top. Nat turned around and lowered herself, to put her feet in his hands so he could ease her descent. Tommy grinned, enjoying the view it gave him up her short skirt. Once he'd supported her halfway down, he told her okay and she turned and jumped the last bit.

"Come on," Tommy said. "We're late."

"Katie won't go anywhere," Chas said with a grin. He took Emma's hand and they jogged off into the woods.

Before long the edifice of the ruined Old Scarston Church rose up, a dark and broken silhouette in the night. They pushed through the trees into the edge of the cemetery, broken headstones overgrown and forgotten. They heard a soft whistle and Katie and Marcus emerged from the trees to their right. This was their spot, their private open-air, night-time clubhouse. Tommy took Katie in a hug and kissed her, Natalie the same with Marcus. Chas and Emma shrugged and set to kissing themselves. For a fair while, all six teenagers lay on the soft ground under the edge of the trees and enjoyed their illicit meet-up. Four Scarsdell Academy students and two Market Scarston village kids enjoying one of their frequent out-of-bounds nighttime rendezvous. Of late, it had become a Friday late-night ritual, a respite from the oppressive private school life.

"This is making me thirsty," Marcus said after a while. "I've got some beers."

"Did you bring any weed?" Katie asked.

Tommy grinned, pulling a small plastic baggie from his pocket. "You know the deal. Village kids bring the booze, and I bring the bud."

"Because you don't have to pay for it," Katie said.

"You're telling me Marcus paid for the brews?"

"No, but I had to steal them. Some of us have to take risks in order to have a good time."

"Hey, I'm taking a risk just being here," Tommy said. He set to rolling a joint while Marcus dug around behind a half-buried headstone near where they'd been waiting and pulled out a six-pack of beer. He handed them around.

"Another one each once these are done," he said.

"I'm cold!" Katie said, huddling close to Tommy. "What'll we do when winter really sets in?"

"Cuddle more?" Tommy said with a grin. She rolled her eyes and he leaned over and gave her a peck on the cheek.

He lit the joint and they passed it around, chattering about nothing in particular, but every subject weighted down with the importance of the world. Everything was simultaneously important and irrelevant to teenagers. Before long they were all riding a happy buzz, the talk slowing down.

"You hear about the old woman in the village, Sapkowsky or Sarkovsky or something?" Marcus asked.

"What about her?" Nat said.

"Dead. Found face down in her back garden."

"Oh, that's horrible," Nat said. "But she was old? Was it a heart attack or a stroke or something?"

Marcus shrugged. "Don't know. But she was found by the postman when he tried to knock to get her to sign for a parcel. When she didn't answer he went to check if she was in the back garden. And she was, half in the flower bed and dead. Now, my dad knows Carl Peters, who knows Steve, the postman. Carl said that Steve told him she had a big gash right across her neck!" He drew one forefinger from ear to ear to emphasize his point, grinning stupidly.

"What?" Katie said. "Why? How?"

"Exactly!" Marcus declared, wiggling his eyebrows. In the gloom of the woods at night his teeth were bright, his excited breath steaming in the chill air.

"If there was a cut across her neck," Nat said, "I bet it wasn't so big as the rumor mill might suggest, and I expect it happened when she fell or something."

"Or maybe Black Shuck got her," Tommy said.

Marcus giggled, but Chas, Nat and Emma looked

confused.

"Don't be daft," Katie said.

"You know about Black Shuck?" Tommy asked. "You should. Very famous around these parts."

"What is it?" Emma asked.

"It's local nonsense," Katie said.

"Oh, no it's not." Marcus sat forward. "The Black Shuck is an omen of death. A giant demon dog, more than seven feet long, he roams the land at night."

Nervous looks and half-smiles were exchanged. Marcus warmed to his audience. "He's a giant of a dog, all black, with wide, tooth-filled jaws. Shuck derives from an Old English word meaning devil or fiend, and a fiend he truly is. One night, nearly five hundred years ago, Black Shuck burst into Blythburgh Church and tore two people's throats out, right in front of the congregation. As they screamed and scrambled to escape, the steeple came crashing through the church roof, brought down by Shuck's evil intent! Known as the Cathedral of the Marshes, it's said that the flagstones of Blythburgh still bears the scorch marks left by Black Shuck's claws. Sometimes, more scorched claw slashes appear randomly on the door of the church, then fade with the dawn."

"Well, I'm glad that was five hundred years ago and long way away," said Nat with a laugh.

"Oh, but that's just it," Marcus said. "Black Shuck is still around. Demons don't die, after all. With his fiery red eyes, he stalks the land to this day. He's been here, in these very woods."

"Nonsense!" Emma said, but her eyes betrayed her fear.

"Oh, it's true. A few years back a couple, probably about the same age as us, snuck out into the woods. Let's be honest, they were here for the same reasons we are. The girl was the only child of a widowed man, and he was strict. He wouldn't let his daughter out at night, wouldn't let her see other people, especially boys. But we all know the appetites of teenage girls!" He grinned at Natalie and she made an outraged face and slapped his arm.

"So, of course, she had a boyfriend in the village," Marcus went on, his voice taking on the cadence of an old storyteller, the tale clearly practiced. "Right here in Market Scarston. And they snuck in here one night, as they had a number of times before. But this night, her father had noticed her leaving. Rather than stop her, the old man decided to follow and scare the living hell out of his daughter and terrify whatever boy was abusing her. So he brought along his shotgun, intending to brandish it at the boy and make sure his point was entirely clear. He followed her into the woods, but he got turned around and lost track of her. Frustrated, he began to retrace his steps when he heard a soul-stilling growl and then a scream. Another scream, a young man yelling, then a blood-curdling howl.

"The girl's father ran toward the sounds, and when he burst into a small clearing, not half a mile from where we sit right now, he found the young man on the ground under the huge paws of a giant black dog with flaming red eyes. His daughter was on the ground not far away, her dress torn and blood on her face. The man wet his drawers, but he fired the shotgun, both barrels right into the giant dog's face. The dog roared, grabbed the obviously dead young man in its huge jaws, and loped away into the darkness of the woods. The man ran to his daughter, but she lived, only fainted. He carried her out of the woods and they moved away the very next day. The young man was never seen again. Sometimes, at night, if you stand still in Market Scarston Square, you can hear a distant howling. And if you listen very carefully, you can hear the young man's wails of agony as he's torn apart again and again."

"Good lord, Marcus, stop it!" Emma snapped.

Marcus sat back, obviously pleased with himself.

Tommy smiled, but chills tickled his veins. He'd heard several legends around Black Shuck and something always gave him pause. It wasn't like other urban legends, too much consistency, too many sightings from people who had no reason to lie. He'd always thought there was some truth to the Black Shuck tales.

"You scared, honey?" Katie said, looking sidelong at him. She slipped an arm around his shoulders and squeezed.

Tommy laughed it off, but Marcus had spooked him. It must have shown on his face. He felt foolish.

"What was that?" Emma said, twisting to look behind her into the darkness of the woods.

"Nothing," Katie said. "Don't let Marcus scare you."

Emma turned up onto her knees. "No, I definitely heard something." As the others began to talk, Emma glanced sharply back. "Hush! Listen."

They fell into an awkward silence, ears straining. Tommy's heart beat faster and gooseflesh stippled the skin of his arms, despite the warmth of his jacket. A twig snapped out in the darkness.

Emma gasped, turned to look at the group again with wide eyes. Tommy's heart beat faster still. Katie's arm around his shoulders tightened. Chas, Nat, and Marcus all looked equally concerned. A low growl sounded, not too far away.

"All right, I know you all heard that!" Emma hissed.

Marcus laughed nervously. "A badger, Em, that's all. Or a fox?"

"We should go," Tommy said.

Chas and Marcus both sneered at him. "You scared, Tommy?"

He frowned, torn between keeping up a strong front and admitting that yes, he was a little concerned.

"I want to go," Katie said, and Tommy was grateful she'd given him an out.

"The girls are spooked," Tommy said. "You shouldn't tell scary stories, Marcus. Come on, we'll walk you two back to the village, then we'll follow the road back to dorms."

"I want to stay," Marcus said. "It's not too late yet."

A crash in the trees behind him made everyone yell and before they knew it, all six were up and running headlong through the woods, away from the sudden disturbance.

"Don't go back into the woods!" Tommy shouted. "Head for Church Lane!" He veered left, and the rest followed like a small, terrified school of fish. Tommy crashed on and a moment later realized Katie wasn't beside him anymore. The group had split up their panic. As he ran, Tommy glanced behind and caught a glimpse of something large and black behind him. It loped on long legs, a shaggy silhouette in the night, except for two glittering points of light. Were they red? Could they be its eyes? Tommy suppressed a sob and ran on, suddenly lost and terrified.

It can't be real, he told himself. *It can't be!*

2

Scarsdell Academy

Jake Crowley startled awake at the incessant banging. His body curled in on itself without conscious thought as his hand reached for a weapon. He turned into a sitting position, unable to find the assault rifle, and something twisted up around his legs. He let out grunt, half fear, half determination. The kind of determination that had kept him alive thus far. Then reality swam back in through his sleep-muddled mind. He was safe, in his bed, in the strange old building in Suffolk.

"You're not in the service any longer. You took a teaching job at Scarsdell Academy," he said aloud, reminding himself his war was over. He wondered if the nightmares would ever end.

The banging was knocking on his bedroom door. He clambered from bed and pulled on a robe calling out, "Just a minute." His voice was thick with sleep. He trudged across the large wood-paneled room on the top floor of the old academy in Market Scarston, on the same floor as the student dorms. He was the newest on staff, after all, and hadn't earned a fancier suite elsewhere like the senior teachers. Which meant he got the privilege of playing babysitter to a horde of teenage boys. He dragged one hand over his face, and opened the door.

Bradley Davenport stood outside in his pajamas. Fourth year, maybe fifth year? Crowley couldn't remember. If he was honest, after the troubles he'd managed to get into following his time in the SAS, he was having trouble adjusting to civilian life. He needed to get his head straightened out.

"You're needed at once," Bradley said.

"What's happening?"

"Tommy is missing, Sir." At Crowley's frown, Bradley said, "Tommy Arundel. Fifth year. Spoiled rich kid."

Crowley nodded, realization dawning. If he were honest, he was neither sorry nor surprised the boy was missing. Arrogant, risk-taker, always looking for trouble. Crowley allowed himself a private smile. Perhaps Tommy Arundel wasn't so different from Crowley himself at that age. "I'll be right down."

Bradley nodded and hurried away. Crowley dressed quickly, then headed down to the common room. As he approached the large, ground-floor room with its couches and leather armchairs, he heard a woman's voice say, "Don't see what you need him for."

Crowley recognized Elizabeth Morgan's voice. From the start she'd made it clear that she didn't like him and he had no idea why. She was a fellow teacher, the newest one before he arrived. Maybe she resented him stealing her baby of the faculty position. Juvenile though he knew it was, he always called her Beth, just to annoy her. When they'd first met and been introduced, he'd said, "Nice to meet you, Beth," and she'd snapped, "Elizabeth, thank you!" It had set the tone for their relationship from that point on. Her room was on the same floor as Crowley's, at the other end of the dormitories. She was the resident advisor. Bradley must have awoken her first, and Crowley wasn't sure why that irked him, but it did.

Morgan fell quiet as he entered, looked away. He managed to give her a smarmy grin before she averted her eyes. Bradley Davenport stood beside her and on her other side was the Headmaster, Archibald Beckett. Ranged nervously in front of the teachers were three more sixth years, Charles Bale, whom everyone called Chas, Nathalie Evans, known as Nats, and Emma Warwick.

"Thank you for joining us," Beckett said. He turned back to the three sixth years. "Now, for the benefit of Mr. Crowley and Ms. Morgan, please tell us what happened."

The teenagers looked nervously at each other. Eventually Nats gave Chas a shove. He nodded quickly, looked at each teacher in turn. "We went out," he said, his voice hoarse.

"Out of bounds? After hours?" Beckett asked, as if to emphasize the illegality of the act.

"Yes, Sir. We went to the village. Just to, you know, hang out."

"Drinking and smoking?" Morgan asked, hands on hips.

Chas reddened, but didn't reply.

"Where did you go exactly?" Crowley asked.

"Old Scarston Church," Chas said. "Well, the woods and cemetery behind the church."

"And then what happened, boy? Spit it out!" Beckett's patience had clearly run out.

Chas startled then spoke rapidly. "We got to telling scary stories and sort of freaked everyone out."

Morgan groaned. "Let me guess. Black Shuck?"

Chas nodded.

"What's that?" Crowley asked.

Morgan looked at him, a half smile tugging one side of her mouth. "I wouldn't expect an outsider to know. Black Shuck is a devil dog that reputedly haunts the region. There are a lot of stories going around, in a few places in Suffolk. All of them nonsense, of course."

Crowley nodded. He had heard some of the legends in the few short months he'd been at Scarsdell, but didn't admit as much. Let Morgan have her moment. Instead, he turned back to the students. "What happened next?"

"After Marcus spooked us, we heard something creeping up through the trees, then growling, then we saw a flash of red eyes," Chas said.

"Oh, come on!" Crowley said. "And you thought it was Black Shuck?"

"It was something!" Emma said, face defiant. "I heard it first, then everyone else did too, then it burst from the trees! It was a huge black dog."

"You're winding us up," Morgan said. "You expect us to believe you actually saw it? What is it you're trying to cover up?"

"Nothing!" all three said in unison.

"Honestly," Chas said. "That's what happened. It was big and had this shaggy fur and–"

"I thought it had shorter fur," Nats said. "But it definitely had red eyes."

"Or sort of orangey-colored," Emma added.

"You can't even agree on what you saw!" Morgan said, exasperated.

"We can agree that we all saw it," Chas said. "And we ran, in a panic, but we got separated. Tommy said to run for the church lane, but there was undergrowth and trees and stuff. We kind of split up, and Tommy was still running the other way and the huge dog went after him! We three met at the academy wall, where we always climb over, and we waited. But Tommy never came back." Chas looked away, guilt and concern written across his face.

Crowley frowned. He wasn't sure what had really happened, but he felt like Chas believed the story he was telling.

"Mr. Crowley," the headmaster said. "I hate to ask, but would you please go out and look for Tommy?"

Crowley looked at Beckett in surprise. "I could, but why not call the police? Isn't this a little serious?"

Beckett flashed a knowing smile. "The boy is probably just lost in the woods, spooked and panicking. No need to notify the police and stir up trouble."

And risk harm to the school's reputation, Crowley thought, but kept that to himself.

"Also," Beckett added, "Tommy's father is an old school chum and one of our most important benefactors. If we can avoid involving the police with his family, that would be better for all." He turned to the three contrite teenagers. "As for you lot, straight back to your beds this instant. You are to report to my office directly after breakfast where you will receive your punishment for breaking quite a few school rules."

The three grimaced, but were wise enough to nod and

keep their silence. They filed out, Bradley Davenport following after a brisk nod from Beckett.

"I'll get a torch and drive around to Church Lane," Crowley said.

"I'm going with you," Beth said, eyes daring him to contradict her.

He smiled. "It's fine, Beth. I've got this."

Morgan rolled her eyes. "Do you even know where the church is, Mr. Crowley?"

Crowley sighed. He sort of knew, but in the dark, perhaps he wouldn't find it so easily. And time was of the essence, in case the boy was hurt. "Fine. But I'll drive."

3

Elizabeth Morgan sat on the fine leather passenger seat of Jake Crowley's British racing green Bentley Mulsanne. The car was a giant luxury cruiser, ostentatious in the extreme and well beyond a soldier's or a teacher's salary. When she'd first seen Crowley driving it, she'd looked it up. Made throughout the eighties, it was an old car, but in beautiful condition. It had a Rolls Royce V8 engine under the bonnet. She desperately wanted to ask Crowley how on earth he had come to own such a car, but she didn't want to give him the satisfaction of not telling her. The man was suspiciously vague about his past. And he would only use it as an excuse to call her Beth again. Only her father was allowed to call her that, and she would continue to insist he use Elizabeth like everyone else

She sneaked a sidelong glance at the man as he drove. He was handsome, around six feet tall, his dark hair cut short and neat. She guessed him to a few years short of her thirty-two, but beyond that she worried about how little they knew about this enigmatic and, frankly, infuriating man. He was strong, well-built under his collared shirt and jacket. Not big like a bodybuilder, but muscular, athletic. Clearly ex-military, that was evident in his manner, his bearing, his neatness, despite his reluctance to share details. And in the wariness he displayed, often on-edge.

Everyone at the academy pretended not to care about Crowley's arrival, but they all whispered about him too. He was a last-minute addition to the faculty, his position endowed by an anonymous benefactor. No one knew for a fact if the benefactor literally bought Crowley's way onto the faculty but it was easy enough to add one and one. Morgan was under no delusions about the favors cast around private schools, but she resented Crowley's seemingly easy pass. She'd worked her arse off to get a position at the prestigious academy. Why hadn't he?

"Earth to Beth!"

She jumped, realized he'd been saying something while she was lost in thought. "Sorry, what?" She bristled at his use of Beth again. "And please, how many times? It's Elizabeth or Ms. Morgan."

"I asked you which way to the old church? I know it's across the village, backing onto the same woods that share the eastern side of the academy."

"Yes. Head right through the village. I'm sure you know the Leaping Hound?"

"I do."

She wasn't surprised he was familiar with the village pub. "Good. Straight past that, then the first lane on the right. I'll point it out. It's easy to miss in the hedgerows."

Crowley directed the Bentley along the narrow lane from the academy and into the village proper. The Tudor houses with their white walls and black wooden beams, thatched roofs, red tiles, and deep curbs were familiar to any English market town. He headed towards the High Street and around the village green in its center. On the left-hand side, the large pub loomed in the darkness.

The Leaping Hound was a two-story building with white walls and lichen-covered red tiles on the roof. It had steep gables, black frames around its sash windows, and a large black wooden door. Several weathered wooden tables and benches were placed on the wide footpath out the front, the pub garden a large green expanse fenced in behind. It was all dark at the late hour, the pub sign with its almost cartoonish leaping black dog shifting gently in a light breeze. On the far side, a gravel car park sat empty.

"Actually," Morgan said, "pull in there."

"The pub car park?"

"Yes. It's a short walk from here past the new church, and maybe that foolish boy is hiding out somewhere along Church Lane. Better we go on foot from here and see if we can find him."

"Is it likely he's lost in the woods?"

"It's possible. The forest is large and sprawls out from the edge of the village. Our academy is on one side, the village perpendicular to that, but on the other two sides it goes on a long way then meets farmland and old family estates. Let's hope we don't have to traipse through there, eh?"

Crowley nodded, pulling into a parking space. "Let's hope."

Morgan sat while Crowley turned off the engine and she nearly asked him about the car. Surely it was a quirk of character to own such a thing, but if she asked, it would be seen as prying. Which, she supposed, is exactly what it was. But she so wanted to know. Perhaps he'd inherited it.

She got out into the cool autumn night, the leafless trees scribbled silhouettes against the stars, and checked her watch. Just after one o'clock in the morning. They should all be in their beds. She for one would be a wreck the next day. Damn that Tommy Arundel.

"At least tomorrow is Saturday," Crowley said, reading her expression. "This way then?" he asked, pointing across the road.

She was about to say yes when three men came along the footpath. They saw each other and the three immediately veered to intercept. She'd seen them around the village, good for nothing, but didn't know their names. They were clearly drunk and the middle one held a bottle of something, half-empty. It looked like whisky.

"Hey hey, lovebirds!" the one with the bottle slurred.

"Come on," Morgan said, and started away from the three men.

Crowley fell into step beside her, but the three weren't planning to give up.

"Oi," said the middle one. "I said hello!"

Crowley turned to face them. "No, you didn't. You made a crack about lovebirds. We're work colleagues and not interested in your games. Go on, off you go."

"Or what?" The man's cronies *hurr-hurred* at this bit of eloquence.

Morgan frowned, hoping Crowley wouldn't stir them up. Was he the sort to start something? She thought maybe he had that potential.

"Tell you what," Crowley said. "Maybe you can help us. Have you seen any students from the Scarsdell Academy around the village tonight? Or around the old church maybe?"

The one in the middle and the one on the left sneered and shook their head. The other one said, "How am I supposed to know if they go to your school?"

Angry looks flashed between the three. "Shut up, Thatch," said the middle one, brandishing the bottle threateningly at his friend.

Thatch frowned and looked away. "Sorry, Rupert."

"So, did you see some kids or not?" Crowley asked.

Morgan watched the belligerent expressions of the three. They would say nothing more unless it was offensive, she thought.

Crowley nodded, smiled. "Well, good. Thanks for your help, gents."

He turned away and Morgan saw a look pass between the three men that Crowley missed. He'd underestimated them. Rupert grabbed her, one arm hard around her throat. His bottle banged painfully into her ribs as he hauled her backwards. Thatch and the other man jumped Crowley.

Struggling to break his chokehold, Morgan had a moment of panic before Crowley sprang into action. He moved with the grace of a dancer, striking out with quick, brutal efficiency. He drove a fist into Thatch's face and Thatch hit the pavement like a sack of butter, blood streaming from his nose. She didn't see what Crowley did next, but a moment later the other man yelped and fell to his knees, rocking side to side, cradling a broken arm.

Crowley turned towards Morgan and her attacker. "Really, Rupert?" he said, not even out of breath. "What are you planning? Robbery? Rape? You think it'll go unnoticed and you'll be all fine once you sober up?" He took a step forward.

Rupert's grip on Morgan vanished and she heard his footsteps slapping the pavement as he bolted away, back toward the village green. Stunned, she let Crowley take her hand and lead her back to the road, heading for the end of Church Lane.

She finally found her voice. "How on earth did you manage that?"

Crowley glanced at her, shrugged. "Years of practice."

4

Old Scarston Church

Crowley gently massaged his knuckles as they walked along the narrow path towards the ruins of Old Scarston Church. He hated to admit it, but he had greatly enjoyed the opportunity to lay waste to some drunken fools. The exercise and the release of tension made his nerves sing, but he figured he'd do well not to let Morgan notice. He was a respectable teacher now, after all, thanks to a few strings pulled. While he might still enjoy some of the old, less respectable, activities, he couldn't let on about it.

They reached the end of the lane and the ruins stood before them, still impressive despite their disrepair. The building retained an imposing air, a sense of purpose. The stones of its construction, rounded by time and weather, were thick and heavy. In places where the walls had fallen, some loose individual stones lay scattered among the long grass and weeds. Stone window frames hinted at the colored stained glass they once contained, now skeletal in silhouette in the moonlight.

"I can see why people come here after dark to give themselves a fright," Morgan said, hugging herself tightly.

"It's just a fallen down old building on the edge of some woods," Crowley said. "What's frightening about that?"

"A church? A cemetery? At night? You don't find that even slightly spooky?"

Crowley shrugged. It was just stone and trees. "Not really. The only people here other than us are dead, and long dead at that. Nothing can hurt us. Those drunk idiots in the street were more dangerous than anything here, assuming a wall doesn't fall on you."

"You're not scared the dead might be restless?" Morgan wore an expression of amusement, but Crowley saw a genuine measure of fear underneath it. She was actually spooked by this place.

"I'm no believer in the supernatural," he said. "I've learned we have a lot more to fear from other people than anything our imagination can conjure up."

Morgan laughed. "You'd be surprised to learn how many of the villagers around here are superstitious. Which can be a frightening thing in its own right, when you think about it."

Crowley couldn't argue with that. He produced a flashlight and shined it around the ruins. Morgan frowned at him, somehow annoyed at his preparedness. She dug in her pocket and pulled out a phone, fired up its flashlight and began looking around too. Crowley smirked, but thought it best not to comment.

The grass and weeds were heavily overgrown, not giving much away. Crowley spotted a couple of places among the old, crooked headstones where it looked like people had sat or lain down. Teenagers enjoying each other's company no doubt. But nothing much could be learned by that. A few beer cans lay scattered in one spot and they seemed shiny and unweathered. Maybe the ones Tommy and his friends had left in their panic earlier. They moved inside the church, shining their lights over the uneven flagstones of the floor. The old altar still stood, cigarette butts and half empty beer cans scattered atop it.

"Bloody hell," Morgan said, half under her breath. "Spoiled rich kids with no respect."

Crowley chuckled.

"You think it's funny?" she asked.

Crowley shook his head. He related, that was all. "It's hard to explain," he said. "Let's look out there on the far side of the cemetery."

Wondering if he'd missed something near the fresh cans he'd spotted before, Crowley went for another look. Something had crashed through the trees, they'd been told earlier. He turned in a half circle, wondering which way the kids might have bolted. He took a few steps in the direction he thought best and soon came to a gap between more trees where the grass wasn't so thick. He found a jumble of fresh footprints in the soft earth.

"Here, look." He shone his torch for Morgan to see. "They were running, heading that way."

"You can't possibly know that," Morgan said, her tone dismissive.

Crowley frowned. Perhaps she needed taking down a peg or two. He understood that she didn't trust him, and he knew her reasons why. They were well-founded, if he were honest. But while his appointment and his history had strings attached, his expertise wasn't up for question, nor were his intentions. "Look at the distance between the prints," he said. "And imagine running compared to walking. Now look at how each impression has a deep toeprint, and faint to no heelprints. That's what tells me they were running. The direction is self-evident. They're clearly fresher than any other marks around here, even the grass still pressed down into a few of them. It hasn't sprung back up yet, which makes these a few hours old at most. If that." He looked at Morgan, one eyebrow raised, challenging her to disagree.

She pursed her lips, then grudgingly nodded. "Yes, fair enough."

"Shall we follow them?"

Morgan couldn't help a half smile tugging at her lips. She was softening to him, perhaps. "Lead on," she said.

They followed the tracks into the forest. It wasn't too hard to see where they went, but soon the way became confused. A jumble of prints told Crowley that the group had paused for a moment, moved back and forth. A single set took off in one direction while the others appeared to double back towards Church Lane.

Crowley pointed it out to Morgan. "I think they realized here they were panicking and headed back towards civilization. But this single set, heading the other way around this dense copse of trees, I'll bet that's Tommy, getting separated from the others."

Morgan grimaced even as she nodded, as if the very act of agreeing with Crowley pained her. He inwardly grinned.

They followed the lone prints deeper into the forest, then out from the gloom of the trees and into the open of rolling fields. With the grass growing again, they lost the trail. The pair traversed the general area, looking for a sign. Finally, Crowley found another footprint.

"Here," he said. He pointed out across the field. "And still running, that way."

They kept moving, sticking to a general direction. Crowley hoped they'd find more prints, because the boy could have veered off in any direction and they might go wildly astray without further clues. Morgan froze, then gasped.

"What is it?" Crowley asked.

She pointed down at the ground. The circle of her phone light wavered as she directed it down onto a patch of soft mud. Crowley moved in and knelt for a better look. He blinked and looked again. It was a giant canine pawprint, pressed deep into the dark mud. Nerves rippled through him. It was the biggest paw print he had ever seen!

5

The Blood Field, Market Scarston

"Okay, let's settle down for a minute," Morgan said, though her tone was anything but settled. "I can't quite believe what I'm seeing here."

Crowley couldn't help the smirk that played across his face. "Quite settled, thank you. Although I can't deny, I'm taken aback by the size of this paw print." He looked around the dark and shadowy field, toward the silhouetted tree line. Surely nothing to worry about, really?

Morgan took a long breath in through her nose, hands on hips. "So, then what happened, Mister Quite Settled Thank You?"

"Let's be rational about this," Crowley said. "Perhaps the kids did get spooked by something, and Tommy did get chased. If that's the case, it was undoubtedly a stray dog. They were drinking and had already unnerved each other with Black Shuck tales. Scaring each other at night is a pastime as old as stories themselves. Coincidence, then, that a stray dog heard them, or sniffed them out. It was probably just coming to beg for food or a pat."

Morgan nodded, lips pursed. She looked around, as Crowley had done moments before. "You're right, of course. Black Shuck is a pervasive myth in these parts and lots of people do insist on entertaining the supernatural, but it is just a myth. Nothing more. The dog surely meant them no harm, as you say. Of course it chased them when they ran. That's what dogs do." She paused, looking down at the shadowy ground again. "But that is an awfully large print."

Crowley, despite his insistence on a rational explanation, privately agreed with her. But he was loathe to admit as much. Whatever left this track was massive. Then again, a dog's paw was prone to spread in order to carry its weight. The print left behind, especially in soft mud like this, often belied the actual size of the dog that left it. But still...

He tore his eyes from the mark and looked out across the night-darkened grass again. "They were heading this way," he said, nodding the direction. They wandered on across the field, eyes scanning for anything that might give them a clue.

After a moment, Morgan asked, "Jake, do you know where we are?"

Crowley smiled inwardly. That was the first time she had ever used his first name. Perhaps she was warming to him, after all. *The old Crowley charm*, he thought sardonically. "I know my socks are getting wet from all the damp grass. That makes it a pretty normal field in that respect. Is there more I should know?"

Morgan smiled, shook her head at his close-to-dad-joke comment. "This is the Blood Field. It's the site where Boudicca and her Iceni tribe met and almost destroyed a detachment of the famed Roman legion, the Ninth, in 60 AD."

Crowley looked at her, genuinely impressed. "Okay, my wet socks be damned, that is an interesting thing to learn. As the history teacher here, I should know that."

Morgan nodded. "Well, now you do. At least, it's one possible site for that particular battlefield."

"Possible site?" Crowley asked. He paused, crouched to brush aside some longer grass, still searching for tracks to follow.

"You know how it is in Britain," Morgan said. "So many stories, so many communities desperate to claim them for themselves. Just think about how many places declare themselves the real location of Camelot, after all."

"Tintagel," Crowley said, decisively. "In Cornwall."

"Sure, that's a favorite, but not ironclad in its claim. Same with the Blood Field here. One set of accounts places the battle firmly here, and that's the one we locals are happy to declare the truth, obviously. But there is another legend that places the battle at Sturmur in Essex." Her tone of voice said all Crowley needed to hear about her opinion of that particular tale. "But there is another legend still, and that one's more problematic. It suggests the battle may actually have taken place just a few miles that way." She pointed off across the field.

"You sound as if that's a problem," Crowley observed.

She nodded. "It is. Because that account places the Blood Field in the rival neighboring village of Wellisle."

"Rival village?" Crowley said with a laugh.

"Don't knock it," Morgan said, though amusement was evident in her tone. "Market Scarston and Wellisle have been rivals for centuries. You should have seen the uproar when Wellisle came second to us in Britain's Prettiest Village back in the early nineties. It was glorious."

"So, what does the archaeological record say?" Crowley asked. "About the real Blood Field, I mean, not pretty flowers on roundabouts."

Morgan flashed him a look that had a genuine edge of resentment in it. "Nothing. No one has ever found a single artifact to confirm or corroborate in any way. Here or in Wellisle," she added. "But we know the true site is this one."

"Perhaps Sturmur has the genuine claim, after all," Crowley said, unable to avoid teasing her. "In Essex."

Morgan made a derisive huff. "There is equally no evidence for that either."

Crowley, scanning the ground still for tracks, spotted a wide spread of darkness just below Morgan's foot. He dove sideways and snatched at her arm at the last instant, just as her foot disappeared into it and she nearly pitched headfirst into the hole.

"What the hell?" Morgan snapped, landing a surprisingly hard punch into Crowley's chest.

He pointed. "You were about to break your neck!" She turned her angry gaze from him to the hole in the field. "You're welcome," he added.

"Oh. Well, thank you."

"You're welcome," he said again, meaning it this time.

They shined their lights down into the hole. It was pitch

black, maybe a couple of feet across with ragged edges. The grass and roots were hanging around the irregular edge of the hole.

"Looks like something's collapsed underneath," Crowley said. "And recently. Though I'm not sure what. Maybe an old cellar, from a building that used to be here, but has long since gone to history. But whatever it was, it's deep."

He crouched, leaning forward to reach his arm into the hole and shine his light further around below ground. The beam cut through darkness and splashed across a figure lying on the floor down below. "Tommy?" Crowley shouted. "Tommy Arundel, is that you?"

The young man looked up groggily, eyes unfocussed, then squinting against the light. "Mister Crowley, Sir?" his voice sounded both scared and hopeful.

"Yes, Tommy, it's me."

Tears escaped over the boy's dirty cheeks and he struggled into a sitting position. "Can you get me out of here?"

6

The Blood Field

Morgan already had her phone in hand, having used the light all the way, so she quickly dialed. Then she frowned at the screen. "Dead zone," she said.

"That's what I used to call my ex," Crowley said before he could stop himself.

Morgan glared at him, but a smile twitched the corner of her mouth.

"Dead fish, she was," Crowley said, grinning. "If the power went out, I used to put perishables next to her to keep them cold."

A laugh escaped Morgan despite her obvious desire to hold it in. She nodded to the hole in the ground. "Shall we help young Mr. Arundel?"

"Certainly."

"Right, well I have no signal. Like so many places around here, this field appears to be a mobile reception dead zone."

Crowley checked his phone and nodded. "Me too." He grinned at her. "Deader than my ex's libido."

Morgan grinned, but looked away. Crowley enjoyed the fact that she was finally being less stuck up around him. He understood her reservations, but he was the kind of guy who wanted to be liked. "What shall we do, then?" she asked.

"Mr. Crowley?" came Tommy's nervous voice from below ground.

"Hang in there, Tommy," Crowley said. "We're figuring out what to do." He turned back to Morgan. "The kid is scared and I don't know that we can get him out too easily. I'll jump down there to be with him. I'll check him out, administer whatever first aid I can. You head back to town and call help. They can get us both out when they get here.

Sound okay?"

Morgan nodded. "Tommy," she called down into the hole. "It's Miss Morgan here. Are you hurt?"

"Can't stand on my ankle, Miss. Might be broken, I'm not sure. Just a bit banged up, I think. Turned my ankle a bit."

"Okay, you just wait there a moment." She stood, looking back to Crowley. "I'll head to the village until I get a signal, then I'll call the headmaster and an ambulance. I can wait by the pub until they arrive and guide them up here."

"Keep an eye open," Crowley said. "In case those drunken idiots come back."

"I think you probably saw them off for the night. Besides, it's that late now that pretty much every local drunk will be passed out somewhere. But yes, I'll be careful."

Without another word she jogged off across the field. Crowley turned his attention back to Tommy. "Scoot over to one side," he said. "I'm coming down."

He shined his light down, making an estimate of the drop. Probably about nine feet at his best guess. A fair drop, but not dangerous with enough care. As Tommy shifted sideways, Crowley tested the edge of the hole, then lowered himself to a sitting position on its edge, his feet dangling down. Keeping his hands planted firmly behind him, he shifted forward, lowering himself as far as possible, then pushed off and dropped the last of the distance. He landed easily, bending his knees into a full crouch to absorb the impact. Still, it sent a shock from his heels up to the base of his skull.

"Hello, Tommy," he grunted, turning to the boy.

Tommy face was dirty, except where the streaks of his tears of relief had cleaned his cheeks. His pleasure at seeing someone, especially a responsible grown-up, was palpable. "It's good to see you, Sir."

"You said you're banged up. Where are you hurt?" Crowley asked.

"My arse is a bit bruised, to be honest. I fell awkwardly."

"Could be much worse," Crowley said with a laugh. "No head injuries? Doesn't feel like anything's broken?"

Tommy didn't seem to hear him. "I was running from Black Shuck, Sir." The fear was back in Tommy's voice.

"Just a dog, son. A big one, I bet, and frightening, but just a dog. You shouldn't have run, you just encouraged it to chase you."

"Not a big one, Mr. Crowley. A *giant* black dog. Huge, it was, with glowing red eyes."

Crowley nodded, figured there was no point in arguing, especially while the lad was spooked and sitting in the dark in the middle of the night. "What is this place anyway?" he asked, to change the subject.

"No idea, it's dark as a crypt."

Crowley shined his torch around, wondering if there might be something they could use to climb out. He quickly saw the place, whatever it might be, appeared to be both ancient and empty. The walls were grey stone, patched in places with pale lichen. Wooden support beams, silvered with age, held up the ceiling. The large room didn't look like a cellar, though, Crowley mused. The floor was made up of flagstones, each a couple of feet square, and a similar gray to the walls. Crowley was no expert, but it all looked to have been cut from the same stuff. Then he noticed a perfect, meter-wide strip down the center where Tommy had landed. The boy had been lying in that dirt when they'd found him. It was probably what had saved him from further injury when he fell, thankfully landing on the dirt and not the hard stone. Iron rings were fixed in the floor at the center of the room on either side of the dirt strip. Tommy watched Crowley shining his light around and his face creased up at the sight of the iron rings.

"What are those?"

Crowley shook his head. "Very odd, that's all I can say."

He moved around the large space, inspecting the stone walls. One spot stood out, slightly different to the rest of the stonework. Crowley ran his fingers over it, noticed its surface seemed smoother, its corners sharper. He rapped on it with his knuckles and the sound rang hollow.

"What is it, Sir?"

Crowley ignored the boy, lost in the excitement of discovery. He tried to get his fingers into the edges of some of the sharper stones, but couldn't. He rooted in his pockets for something to use, but had nothing on him. Frustrated, he leaned back, lifted one knee, and kicked it. The fake wall shattered, revealing a low passageway beyond.

"Bloody hell, Sir!"

Crowley grinned back over his shoulder. "Interesting, don't you think? Wait there a moment."

Tommy rolled onto his hands and knees. "No way. I don't want to be left alone again. I can't stand, but I can crawl."

"All right, then." Crowley crouched, crab-walking along the low passageway, Tommy crawling close behind. It followed a slow, gradual ascent until they reached a dead end. Crowley tried to estimate if it had risen enough to be back at ground level, but he had no way of working that out.

Shining his light around the end revealed a detailed and colorful mosaic of a bull and a sunburst. Crowley was no archeologist, but it was obviously incredibly old. He took out his phone and snapped a couple of photos, then tried to see if there was a door or a false wall. It had no edges or gaps he could discern. With a shrug, he hammered on it, yelled out, but heard nothing in response.

"Sir, we should go. I don't think we should be here at all."

"Why so agitated, Tommy? It's all right, the ambulance will be here soon, we just have to crawl back the way we came."

Tommy smiled, but didn't seem at all reassured. Crowley tried to have another look at the mosaic, but Tommy tapped him nervously on the shoulder.

"Sir, I don't like it here, can we go back?"

"You go, I won't be long."

"No, Sir, I don't want to be on my own either."

Crowley sighed. The boy was thoroughly spooked. It

was very late, he supposed, and Tommy had had a hell of a fright, and a fall, and he was hurting. Perhaps Crowley ought to pay more attention to his duty of care here, and less to his curiosity. This place wasn't going anywhere, after all. "Okay, Tommy, you lead the way back. I'm right behind you."

As they emerged back through the shattered fake wall into the open room, Crowley heard voices. A moment later, Morgan was at the hole above them.

"Help is here," she called down.

It only took a few minutes for the emergency services, an ambulance, a police officer, and the fire brigade it turned out, to lower a harness down and haul both Tommy and Crowley back up into the field. Archie Beckett, the headmaster, was there as well, eyebrows cinched together. Whether in concern or disapproval, Crowley wasn't sure. Probably both, he decided.

"Funny sort of place down there," Crowley said. He described the room with the strange dirt strip through it, and the ancient mosaic at the end of the short passage. "You ever hear of such a thing around here?"

Beckett shook his head. "Damned mysterious, you ask me. How the hell did you even end up down there, boy?"

Tommy looked abashed, but told his story. It was obvious the police officer and the headmaster were both skeptical about it all, even the alleged dog prints.

"Well," Morgan said, though she sounded reluctant. "Mr. Crowley and I both saw very large dog's paw prints too."

"Really?" Beckett said, one eyebrow raised.

They retraced their steps while the ambulance officer checked Tommy's ankle. Despite looking several times, the prints they saw were nowhere to be found.

"I think everyone has had a late night and enough excitement," the police officer said through his large moustache. "Perhaps it's time everyone was getting back to their beds."

"Well past time," the headmaster agreed. He took

charge of Tommy and excused himself.

As everyone began to disperse, Crowley gestured to Morgan and they moved aside. "What do you think happened to that paw print?" Crowley asked.

An uncomfortable expression passed over the woman's face. "I don't know. Maybe it just…" She shrugged. "I don't know," she said again.

"You heard me describing the mosaic I found?"

She nodded.

"Does that mean anything to you? Ring any bells?"

"It sounds Roman, but as far as that particular symbol, I'm not sure. I don't think so."

Crowley pulled out his phone, showed her the screen. "I didn't tell them but I took a couple of photos. Not the greatest images, being dark down there and the flash on these things leave a lot to be desired, but you can see something of what it was like."

Morgan looked at the phone for a moment, then nodded. "Send me the photos. I'll do some checking."

Crowley knew he wasn't her favorite person, though she had softened somewhat over the course of the evening. He decided he could probably trust her. "Thanks. I'll send them when we get back to the school."

7

Market Scarston

Saturday morning arrived, crisp and bright with the pale blue sky and scudding clouds so common to autumn. Crowley stretched, looking from his window out across the school grounds, damp with early dew. It would be a fine weekend and while he had a lot of marking to do, and planning for the following week, his immediate concerns were focused well beyond the school walls.

He dressed in shorts and a t-shirt, put on a pair of running shoes, and packed a small backpack. Then he headed downstairs for a quick, light breakfast and a strong coffee. He was exhausted after being out so late, but a lie in until eight a.m. was all he allowed himself.

He avoided as much conversation as possible and slipped out with a minimum of fuss. At the school gates he had a cursory warm-up, then began jogging. After the fitness regime of the Army, it was hard to maintain the levels of physical ability he was used to. But frequent running and visits to the gym to lift weights helped, and it also helped his worries. He'd brought a lot back with him from the Middle East. A lot of it he got out of his system in the wild couple of years since he had returned to England and quit the SAS. But that had nearly landed him in jail and, on more than one occasion, nearly killed him. Ironic, considering what he'd survived to get to that point. But he'd been lifted out of that frying pan and helped into the relative calm of the Scarsdell Academy. He smiled. "Thanks, Auntie," he muttered under his breath.

But even now, he carried a lot with him. He knew it was PTSD, along with a cocktail of other, less immediate issues. But he had coping mechanisms too. He wouldn't be too proud to see a counselor again if he felt himself sliding back into old, bad habits. But rigorous physical activity was a great healer, of body and mind. He ran harder, drove his heart rate up. He also had somewhere to be.

It didn't take long to reach the old church ruins, even running the long way around. Torn between pushing himself further and investigating more, he decided the situation of the night before was more urgent. He'd go to the gym at the Academy later in the day and make up for the short run. In truth, anything less than ten miles was a short run in his book, but that was SAS training for you.

He started at the spot where the teenagers had met the night before. Paying closer attention to where the chase had started, Crowley realized there were two further sets of prints, heading back towards the village. Perhaps those were the friends the students had said they'd come to meet. He lost that trail as soon as it reached the lane heading back toward the pub. There was nothing else of particular interest, and he couldn't find any more dog tracks, in the cemetery or in the immediate woods near where the kids had hung out.

He retraced his steps from the night before, back out over the field, but couldn't find any of the dog's pawprints. He shifted grass around, frowning. Even the one he and Morgan had most definitely seen previously, gone like it was never there. It didn't make sense.

A creeping sensation tickled the back of Crowley's neck and he stood quickly, turned around. No one was there. But he had the distinct sensation of being watched. With the amount of time he'd spent in various theatres of war, Crowley had long since learned to trust his sense, trust his gut.

He crouched again, eyes narrowed against the bright spring sunshine, watching the trees. The day had begun to warm up, maybe summer was closer than he'd thought. After a minute or two, he gave up waiting. The sense of someone watching persisted, but there was nothing to see.

With a sigh, Crowley stood and stalked across the grass to the hole in the ground where Tommy had fallen the night before. This time, he'd come prepared. He pulled off his backpack and took out a short coil of rope tied tightly to a grappling hook. The hook was usually used for climbing rocky or frozen mountains, a hobby he'd found as another coping mechanism, but it would also do a fine job of securing the rope to the earth outside the hole, as long as Crowley dug two of its points in deep enough and at an oblique enough angle. He'd collected all kinds of gear since leaving the army, always on the lookout for more adventure. It was hard to replace the adrenaline rush of being shot at. While he would gladly never experience being shot at again, civilian life did get boring quite frequently. He paused, looking at his rope and hook set ready in the middle of a rural English field and couldn't help a small laugh escaping. What was he even doing? Perhaps he should just go to the gym now and exhaust himself with weights. But he really wanted another look at the subterranean chamber and that strangely beautiful mosaic. He yanked on the rope again, double checking that the hook was firmly embedded, then slipped over the edge of the hole and lowered himself the short distance to the dirt strip between the flagstones.

With the bright sunlight streaming in through the hole above, it was much easier to see the details of the chamber. The stone walls and wooden support beams were well-constructed, and old. A cracked stone and fresh earth and grass showed where the roof had fallen in, probably as Tommy ran over it the night before. He assumed it had been weak for some time and only required weight at just the right spot to give way. Unlucky for Tommy Arundel.

The place was quite old, almost certainly from the era of Roman occupation. Crowley investigated the dirt strip and the embedded iron rings, but could make no more sense of them in the shafts of light than he could in the darkness the night before. Regardless, he took numerous photographs from as many different angles as possible.

Then he crawled back up the low passage, determined to get better shots of the mosaic at its end. But the mosaic was gone. And beyond where it had been the passage continued a short way until it ended in piles of rubble. Frowning, Crowley felt around the edges, shined his torch closely to see what had happened. Sharp, straight cuts in the tunnel wall indicated to him that the mosaic had been removed, and quickly, without much care taken. Had the passageway beyond it always been collapsed, or had whoever had taken the mosaic also blocked any further way forward?

Crowley pushed in past the edges of where the mosaic had been and tried to clear the rocks and earth out of the way, but quickly gave up. The collapse was total and there would be no way through without some heavy machinery. And there was certainly no room for that.

But disturbing the rubble had given rise to a faint whiff of a chemical odor. It triggered memories and nerves through Crowley's body, set his hands shaking slightly. He recognized it instantly. Explosives like C-4 were uniquely encoded with materials or chemistries virtually impossible to duplicate. Called an odorizing taggant, they acted like a fingerprint, a unique signature of identity. Taggants were sometimes covert, likely only recognizable by a trained bomb squad dog or specialized technology, but some were overt like this one. Used for a wide variety of applications, they were often employed as a way of tracking bombs and munitions back to the manufacturer. Whoever had used explosives down here probably didn't know anything about that, but Crowley was now certain that the collapse was both intentional and recent. Probably as recent as the early hours of this morning. What the hell was going on here?

Head swimming with confusion, trying to figure out who would do this and why, Crowley crawled back into the main chamber. As he stood in the wan light, he saw his rope shifting side to side. Was someone up there? He opened his mouth to call out when the rope dropped loosely through the hole.

"Hey!" Crowley yelled. "There's someone down here, what are you doing?"

Something else fell through the hole and clattered onto

the flagstones. Something small and rounded. Crowley's eyes widened in horror as he recognized it for an old-fashioned grenade.

8

Natural History Museum, London

Rose Black sat back in her chair in a lower basement room of the Natural History Museum and cursed aloud. There was no one else around to hear her after all, on her own at work on a Saturday morning, again, stuck at a half-sized desk in a forgotten corner, surrounded by junk.

Nearly nine months since she'd landed her dream job, and the dream was looking more and more like a nightmare. There was no doubt she was firmly at the bottom of the pecking order, and things didn't look likely to change. So far she had done a lot of fetching and carrying for senior employees, and fended off the advances of three different married superiors. She'd just about had it.

Her mother, in classic immigrant Chinese fashion, had railed at her for being impatient. Told her she needed to buckle down for years and earn her place. Men would be men and too many women torpedoed their own careers with a refusal to ignore a playful slap or a harmless flirt. Rose loved her mother dearly, but the woman drove her to distraction with her unacceptable views, shaped by generations of misogyny.

Rose refused to put up with it. She looked at the formal complaint form sitting on her small desk, that she had yet to file, and felt shame with herself. For all her moralizing, she hadn't lodged the form yesterday like she had planned to and wondered if she actually would. It wasn't that she agreed with her mother, nothing could be further from the truth, but she did want to keep this job. Although only if the job was the one advertised, that she'd applied for and won fairly.

Another week, she told herself. Sit on the report about sexual harassment from Professor Blake and his wandering hands for one more week and see if she could be given some proper research projects and maybe even get shown a little respect. She ate the last of the sandwich she'd brought to work with her and then turned back to the old records she was filing. Her phone rang. It startled her. Had it ever rung before?

"This is Rose Black."

"Oh, thank God!" the voice on the other end said with a sigh of relief. "I'm glad to finally be talking to a person not an automated menu. My name is Elizabeth Morgan. I'm a faculty member at Scarsdell Academy, over in Suffolk."

"Okay," Rose said tentatively. She'd never heard of the school in question and had no idea why the woman might be calling her. "What can I do for you?"

"Well, I've spent all morning trying to find someone who might be able to help me identify a strange find a colleague and I stumbled onto last night. We made what you might call an unusual archaeological discovery."

Rose immediately perked up. This was exactly the kind of stuff she'd hoped to investigate in her new position. Assuming this Elizabeth Morgan wasn't a crank, of course. The woman might have dug up an old plate in her garden and got over-excited. Rose reminded herself to maintain a professional calm and said, "And how would you describe this discovery?"

"Well, it's in a field in the country not far from the Academy. Some ground has fallen in and there's a chamber underneath, quite large. But the main thing is that along a small passage off this chamber is a mosaic. It's certainly very old. I have some photographs and I did some preliminary investigations. I'm fairly convinced it's Roman. But I quickly ran out of avenues to investigate further and decided I needed some professional help. I've been phoning around for the last two hours trying to find that help. Could it be you, by any chance?"

Rose smiled to herself. Maybe this was finally her chance to do something of value, to get noticed.

"Well, I don't know for sure, Ms. Morgan. But I can

certainly try. Why don't you send me those photographs?"

9

Market Scarston

Instinct took over and Crowley scrambled back up the passageway on hands and feet, his back scraping painfully against the low ceiling. The concussive blast of the grenade's detonation threw him flat, deafened him, and showered him with grit and dust. Stunned, lying on the hard ground, his ears whined in protest. Flashes of insurgents fighting their way out of houses in Afghanistan crossed his mind's eye. His gut went watery at the memories, at the wounds he'd taken, even worse that he'd inflicted. He saw the beautiful young girl, her eyes wide in fear, as she walked out towards them, hands up, lips parted. He heard Peterson yelling that she was strapped, meaning she had a suicide vest on under her long dress. Gunfire, but too late, the blast and flash of detonation, the wind of the explosive outburst, showering them all with sand. Peterson's screams as shrapnel pierced him. Crowley gasped, but couldn't hear his own breathing. His breath was shallow and panicked, his heart hammering hard enough to taste.

"Not anymore," he said aloud, though he couldn't hear that either. "Not there anymore."

He twisted into a sitting position, ran hands over his legs, hips, butt, checking for blood. He'd been hammered with gravel like buckshot, but didn't seem to be wounded. His ears hummed and he spoke again, testing, but still he was deafened by the blast. A blast that had nearly killed him. What the hell was going on here? If someone was still up there, calling down to him or asking questions, he couldn't hear them.

Cautiously he crept forward again. If they'd dropped a grenade it was entirely possible they had a gun too. And who on earth had grenades in rural England? What kind of nutter carried one as a matter of routine? Especially an old one like that. The thing had looked like a WWII relic.

Then again, maybe whoever had been in and removed the mosaic, then collapsed the tunnel beyond it, had also planned to come back and finish the job. Maybe they'd intended to take down the entire chamber, then perhaps bulldoze earth over the top, remove all trace. And they'd discovered Crowley's rope and decided to remove him as well.

His rope! He'd seen it fall in, which meant he was trapped underground for the second time in less than twelve hours. At the mouth of the tunnel, the room was a lot brighter, the hole above blown out to twice its size. Still, it was too high to be reached. Several wooden beams had split and fallen crooked, a number of flag stones upended and cracked. Crowley saw no movement above him and slowly emerged, brushed himself off. Despite the damage, there was no way up and out. Maybe he could stack up some of the broken pieces, make a pile high enough to jump up and grab the edge?

Then he spotted a gap in the opposite wall. The explosion had blown out several stones and a dark space loomed beyond. He hurried over, pulling at more of the stones that had been loosened but not fallen. It took some effort, but he was thankful for the many hours in the gym which meant he was strong enough to pull away more blocks of stone and make a hole big enough to crawl through.

He climbed into another small passageway, similar to the one on the other side. He followed it and it soon opened into a bigger tunnel, and what appeared to be a stretch of old sewer system. It was probably Roman, he mused, given the materials used. With nowhere else to go, he followed it. Before long it opened onto a more modern sewer, though it seemed unused. Perhaps he should be thankful for that.

Then he met another dead end. Frustrated, he shone his torch around and spotted a narrow crack that led to another opening. The wall was solid, but he could see a large space beyond it, if only he could get through. The crack was almost big enough if he sucked in his chest and pushed hard.

He had made it halfway when the stone crushed against his sternum, ground hard against his tailbone, wedging him in tightly. Panic welled up inside him, spots before his eyes, his breath forced too shallow by the restriction of his chest. He couldn't breathe, couldn't take any breath, even a tiny sip of air. He pushed away, trying to go back to where he'd come from, but he was jammed fast, immobile in both directions.

With a gasp of sheer horror, Crowley closed his eyes. Another flash, another hot and dusty day in Afghanistan, chasing insurgents into a system of caves in the hills behind Kandahar. They'd all slipped through a narrow crack and he'd tried to follow, got caught by his webbing despite shucking off his pack as he'd chased them through the cave. But he'd had a knife, managed to angle it back in one hand and cut away the webbing that had him hooked up. The bad guys were long gone by the time he'd got free, but the panic had been real. And now here he was, wearing only shorts and a t-shirt, nothing to cut free and no knife even if there was.

"Calm down, soldier," he said aloud. His hearing was coming back, he realized, his words muffled but audible. He said it again, "Calm down, soldier. Panic is what gets you killed."

Despite being unable to draw a deep breath, despite the dizziness from lack of oxygen and adrenaline surging through him, Crowley willed his body to relax. He started at his head, released the tension from his face, then neck and shoulders. He mentally forced the muscles of his chest and stomach, butt and legs to soften. The pressure eased slightly. He cautiously took a breath, a little deeper than before, then went through the relaxations again. He calmed, and gently pushed himself towards the room he'd seen beyond the crack, forcing himself to stay relaxed. He skinned his chest and his lower back, grazes that burned and would be scabbed and uncomfortable for a week or two, but he slipped through and dropped to his knees in a dusty, low-ceilinged, cement-floored room.

A short flight of wooden steps led to a trap door above him. He put his back to it and pushed hard. It creaked once, twice, then he lowered himself and drove his upper back into the wood and it cracked and popped open. A dank, moldy smell hit him immediately.

Shining his torch around he saw he was in an old cellar. Moldering boxes of old business records, odds and ends, forgotten junk. Some of the boxes bore the words Leaping Hound in looping black pen. Crowley chuckled. This must be the cellar of the local pub.

More stairs, these in better condition, led up from the opposite side of the large cellar. In between were boxes and crates, barrels of beer hooked up to hoses which would lead to the pumps on the bar above.

Crowley went up the stairs and cracked the door an inch. Light flooded in and a surprised-looking man spun around, right on the other side. He was in his fifties or so, balding, a tough-looking character. He grabbed the door and wrenched it all the way open.

"What the bloody hell do you think you're doing?"

10

The Leaping Hound Pub

Crowley tried to adopt an embarrassed expression. "I'm so sorry! I came in here looking for a loo." He gestured to his dirt and dust-covered clothing. "Took a bit of a tumble out jogging and wanted to clean up. I'm not sure how I ended up here. I'm a bit disoriented, if I'm honest."

The gruff man frowned, clearly suspicious. "Didn't see you come in."

Crowley shrugged. "Again, sorry. But if you could tell me the way?"

The man turned and pointed down a short corridor. "To the end, Gents is on the left."

"Thank you!"

Crowley hurried away before the fellow could think too much more about it. His story was obviously untrue, but then again, what else could the man assume? He was quite unlikely to guess that Crowley had squeezed into his basement from forgotten underground passageways.

He found the Gents and washed his hands and face, patted himself down. By the time he finished, he looked more or less presentable, even if he was a little incongruous in his shorts and t-shirt. He went back out and walked through into the pub's main room. The man who had initially confronted him stood behind the bar, pouring pints for a couple of locals. Crowley checked the time. Just after eleven in the morning. The start of a good Saturday lunchtime drinking session for locals with nothing better to do.

As Crowley pasted on a smile, about to excuse himself and leave, something caught his eye. Further along the bar a big, skinhead-looking, middle-aged man was talking animatedly with a red-haired fellow whom Crowley recognized—one of the thugs from the night before. The one who'd grabbed Morgan, then run away after Crowley dispatched his mates. Crowley racked his brain, then the name popped up. Rupert, that was it.

As Crowley made the realization, the large, shaven-headed man turned and walked right up to him. "My son says you beat him up last night."

Crowley gave a half smile. "Not true. I beat up two of his friends, but Rupert ran away before I got a chance to punch him as well."

The man's face clouded like a storm. "You think you're a tough guy?" he demanded, teeth bared.

The bar fell into a tense, expectant silence, everyone paying close attention. Deep down, Crowley realized he was craving violence. He wanted to fight again, especially as this big brute outweighed him and stood a few inches taller. It would be sweet to lay out such a monster of a man. But that desire for violence both frightened and angered Crowley. He still had deep-seated issues to work through. He also needed to keep the peace, despite his craving for blood. He felt as though this man would respond better to strength than debate.

He stepped up, stretching his neck so that they now stood nose to nose. The man gave way a step, a flash of doubt across his face. He was obviously accustomed to intimidating people, instilling fear.

In a quiet, icy voice, Crowley said, "Your son and his two friends attacked me and the woman I was with late last night. Unprovoked. I was defending us."

"That's not how I heard it," the man sputtered.

"Then you heard wrong. After all, Rupert is hardly going to admit he started the trouble, is he?" He closed the space between them a little more. "Are you and I going to have a problem, too? Or am I going to buy a round for the house, like any good neighbor, and we'll forget this whole misunderstanding?"

The man frowned, glanced back at his son. Rupert stared at the beer-stained bar, refusing to meet his father's gaze. The big man turned back. "I suppose I can't deny my friends a free round. Very kind of you." He relaxed and stepped back.

Crowley smiled to the barman, told him to pour for everyone. There were only eight or nine others in the pub along with Rupert, his father, and Crowley himself. A dozen pints was a small price to pay to de-escalate a volatile situation. And he supposed he had to start interacting with the civilian world sooner or later. The private school, while hardly a military atmosphere, made it easy for Crowley to remain disengaged from society.

Once the drinks were served, the tension in the pub eased considerably, but it was clear that everyone was still uncomfortable. Lots of sidelong glances singled Crowley out. It was plain for all to see that he wasn't of their social class, a teacher at the Academy among honest village folk. He ignored it, tried to behave naturally. After a few minutes, as the tension drained further away, various conversations in the place started up again.

An old man, wispy gray hair sticking out all around his flat tweed cap, moved over to the bar and nodded. "You're up at the school, eh?"

"Yes. Jake Crowley." He stuck out a hand to shake.

"Ian Barnes," the old man said, clasping Crowley's hand. His palm was dry and calloused, rough as sandpaper. "How did you get so dirty then? Even cleaned up you're still grubby."

Maybe he hadn't done such a good job in the bathroom after all. The barman had sidled over, one ear tipped their way. Crowley figured the discovery of the strange chamber was no longer a secret, the gossip surely right across the village by now. Maybe he'd learn more if he came clean.

"Did you folks hear about the student who fell in a hole last night?"

Barnes laughed and nodded. "Oh yeah, lot of commotion in the wee hours."

Several others stopped talking to listen in.

"Well, it was me and another faculty member who

found him," Crowley said. "Damn fool teenagers sneaking out in the middle of the night. Anyway, I was out for a run this morning and thought I might go back and have another look. Turns out I'm nearly as foolish and just as clumsy. Took a spill myself."

"Interesting you found that place," Barnes said. "Our village is full of old, hidden archeological wonders."

"Well, technically it was Arundel who found it," Crowley said with a laugh.

"Tommy, eh? Philip Arundel's son." Barnes kept his voice deliberately neutral, then he sneered a little. "I'm sure his Lordship will be proud."

Crowley nodded, non-committal. No doubt a lot of the village held the rich and influential Arundels in higher disdain than Academy teachers.

"Anyway," Barnes said, his tone clearly deflecting the conversation a little. "More proof the battle of the Blood Field did happen in Market Scarston, no? And not in Wellisle." He spat the name of the rival village like a curse.

"I've never been over to Wellisle," Crowley said.

"Arrogant, snobbish, wealthy, always looking down on Market Scarston." Barnes took a long draught from his pint of bitter, then looked up again. "They're almost as bad as those toffs up at the school." He flashed an apologetic look, but Crowley waved it off. "I don't mean all the teachers, of course. Just Arundel and his lot. Arundel is the largest benefactor, after all. He basically runs the place, but I 'spect you know that."

"You don't think Headmaster Beckett has autonomy to run the school?" Crowley asked. Suddenly this casual conversation had become incredibly interesting.

"Archie Bucket, you mean?" someone behind Crowley said. A ripple of laughter ran around the pub.

Barnes grinned, then saw Crowley's frown. "Bucket because all he does is fetch and carry for Arundel."

Crowley frowned. "I was under the impression that Beckett and Arundel were old friends."

Barnes shook his head. "That's the public face of it, but

Bucket has been Arundel's lackey forever. Since their days in that damned history club up at the school as teenagers."

Crowley made a mental note to look into the history club and see what he could learn. He was tempted to ask more of the locals, but knew if he pushed too hard, word would get back to the school that he'd been gossiping in the village. He needed to avoid that.

"Those kids last night thought they were running from Black Shuck," he said, to change the subject. "Talking of village history and all."

"Is that so?" Barnes seemed amused, but there was an edge of seriousness around his eyes.

Crowley remembered Morgan saying how many local folk still believed the old legends. "Any problems with stray dogs in the area?" Crowley asked.

"If you want to know about dogs, talk to Millie Egerton," Barnes said with a note of finality.

Crowley downed the last of his pint. "Okay, I might do that. Thanks for your time. I'd best be getting back."

As he turned to leave, the barman caught his eye. He reached over and shook Crowley's hand. "Jack Boles," he said. "Thanks for calming that situation down earlier, I appreciate you not making more trouble."

"I'm sure no one really meant any harm." Crowley remembered his own brief bloodlust, but pushed it aside.

"Well, thanks all the same. These village lads aren't bad boys, they just can't handle their drink."

Crowley wanted to lecture the man on the nonsense of "boys will be boys" culture and how dangerous it was, but this probably wasn't the time. He just nodded instead, went to turn away.

"Watch yourself up at the school," Boles said quietly.

Crowley paused. The man's tone had struck a chord. This sounded like something that went deeper than simple class resentment. "Why is that?"

Boles shrugged. "Maybe it's just local superstition, I don't know. But the place has a bad reputation. You're new, so still finding your way. Just watch your step, especially around the old boys."

Crowley nodded again. "I will. Thanks for the warning."

He left the pub, mulling over all he'd heard. But something twisted in his gut, some disquiet, uncertain feeling. He saw two middle-aged men at a corner table eyeing him balefully as he walked out. He kept going, keen to avoid any further confrontations.

11

Market Scarston

Crowley headed back to the academy, showered, changed, then ate a sandwich. A little after midday he went down to the student lounge and checked in on the renegades from the night before. They were suitably contrite, Tommy not quite meeting Crowley's gaze.

"How are you feeling today?" Crowley asked.

Tommy made a rueful face. "Not bad. A bit sore is all."

Crowley nodded. "That's good. Any of you know someone called Millie Egerton?" he asked casually.

"She's a dog breeder," Chas said. "Lives across the village." He told Crowley the name of the lane. "Why are you interested in that crazy old lady?"

"Crazy?" Crowley asked.

Chas half smiled, shrugged one shoulder. "I don't actually know her. That's what people say, is all."

"Maybe lay off the gossip then," Crowley said, and left the teenagers to it.

He drove across the village and up the narrow lane to Egerton's house. The place was neat, and quintessentially English. A small stone cottage with a tiled roof, a low stone wall around a neat garden with flowers in tidy beds. Ivy ran up one side of the cottage towards an ornate, twisted pottery chimney. It looked like a chocolate box image, or a thousand-piece jigsaw puzzle. On one side a gravel driveway ran past the house and set a little back were a number of large wired enclosures, each with a big covered kennel at the back. Several dogs paced in their cages.

Crowley parked and went up to the front door. The knocker was a brass Alsatian. He knocked, but got no reply. "Hello?" he called out. "Ms. Egerton?"

Nothing. A couple of the dogs began barking. He

walked around the cottage and along the driveway past the kennels. There were some large, ferocious-looking beasts among them, some well-behaved, but others barked and growled angrily. A couple even snarled at him and charged the fence. Crowley instinctively skipped backward, even though he thought he could probably trust the chain link. One big, furious-looking hound stood, put its front paws on the wire and boomed angry barks at him, teeth bared. It would have had its paws on his shoulders were it not for the enclosure holding it back. Did Egerton deliberately train aggressive dogs?

Crowley circled the kennels and headed back toward the front of the house, thinking maybe he'd come back another time. As he cleared the side of the cottage, a big, black dog, entirely unconstrained, came charging at him. His heart hammered, but he sucked in a breath and stood his ground, knowing not to show fear. He kept his face and demeanor as neutral as possible. The dog let out a low growl as it bounded forward, and Crowley braced, one arm coming up involuntarily in front of his face.

"Hold!"

The voice was sharp and powerful. The dog skidded to a halt and sat, staring at Crowley as it panted gently. An older woman, her hair more gray than brown, deep lines around her mouth and eyes, came around from the other side of the cottage behind the dog. As she drew near, Crowley revised his opinion. Not old, probably no more than fifty at most, but she appeared worn down, aged beyond her years.

"He won't hurt you," she said. Her voice sounded as tired as her face looked. "Jackie!" The dog stood and moved to stand beside her left leg, still keeping its attention on Crowley.

Crowley was accustomed to trained dogs. He'd seen amazing animals in the military, but this one particularly impressed him. Its immediate responses, alert eyes and complete focus. He couldn't help but wonder if it could be trained to chase people on command.

"I'm Jake Crowley," he said. He moved forward to offer his hand, but Jackie growled, low and menacing. Crowley stopped where he was, smiled. Egerton said nothing. "I wanted to have a word with you. Some of the locals said you might be able to help me."

Still Egerton didn't reply, just looked levelly at him.

Okay, Crowley thought. This might be a one-sided conversation. "I'm a teacher up at Scarsdell Academy." Egerton's face tightened. "Some of our students got chased by a large dog last night and I wanted to ask you about it." At her frown he quickly added. "I'm not suggesting it was your dog, only that you're the authority on dogs in these parts."

She stared at him, her expression blank, her eyes flat. Crowley expected her to refuse.

"Come inside." The woman turned and led the way to the house. Crowley followed, keeping one eye on Jackie, but the dog sat where it was and watched him go by. It didn't move a muscle, disturbing in its utter stillness. As Crowley moved around the dog to follow Egerton, he saw a pawprint it had left behind in the mud at the edge of the tidy lawn. This dog was big, but the print it left was half the size of the one he'd seen the night before. This certainly wasn't the dog that had chased Tommy. And none of the other dogs he'd seen were any bigger than Jackie.

Egerton left the front door open, so Crowley left it that way too and followed her into a small sitting room. The place was tidy, brightly lit by large windows, and crammed with stuff. Photographs of Egerton kneeling beside a wide variety of dogs hung from the walls. Ceramic dogs lined the mantle over the fireplace, which was neatly stacked with wood ready for when winter came around again. Sitting in an overstuffed armchair by the fireplace was a huge, black, stuffed dog.

"Tea?" Egerton's face was polite, but it seemed she was simply going through the motions of civility.

Crowley had the feeling she couldn't wait for him to leave, but he wanted to ask his questions. "Yes, thank you."

She turned and headed into the kitchen at the back of the cottage. She wasn't the chattiest person, but if she lived with only her dogs, she probably didn't have many opportunities for conversation. He wandered back out into the hallway and looked at more photos of Egerton with dogs. Next along was a dining room and he poked his head in and saw the table had been set for three. Two seats were already occupied by stuffed dogs. The china was dog-patterned, more similar crockery on display in a glass-fronted cabinet. The Dogs Playing Poker painting hung from one wall, Dogs Playing Pool on the other. He began to understand why Chas had called her a crazy old lady, but she wasn't that old and he was almost sure she wasn't crazy either. Everything about the house had the hint of loneliness about it. He felt sorry for her, then wondered if that was judgmental. It was possible she was entirely happy with her living arrangements. Her annoyance at his presence would seem to back that assumption up.

"It will be a few minutes," Egerton called from the kitchen. "I haven't had guests for... for a long time."

"No worries," Crowley said. "Take your time. I'm in no hurry."

Back in the hallway, he looked up a stairway leading to the second floor. The walls of the stairs were lined with framed awards from dog shows, numerous rosettes and medals hung among them. Crowley slowly wandered up, reading the certificates. Best in Show was frequent. Best Agility was almost as numerous. He found himself on the landing at the top of the stairs, saw there were two bedrooms and a bathroom. Curious, he peeked into one room. It appeared to be Egerton's. More dog photos on the walls, but thankfully no dogs in the bed, stuffed or otherwise. An old framed family photo stood on the bedside table. He squinted, not quite daring to actually go into the room. The photo showed a younger Egerton, and presumably her husband and son. He wondered where they were now.

He turned, nudged the door open of the other

bedroom. It was obviously a teenage boy's room. Football posters from Ipswich Town F.C., a poster of a shapely blonde woman in a bikini, *Star Wars* movie posters. A large, stuffed Dalmatian sat at a small desk. The dog wore a shirt and tie that Crowley immediately recognized as the Scarsdell Academy uniform.

A photo on the desk displayed a teenage version of the young boy in the photo on Egerton's bedside table. In this picture, the young man was clad in an Academy uniform and stood with his arms draped over the shoulders of two more students.

"That's Eric," a voice said from behind him.

Crowley jumped, turned to face Egerton. "Sorry, I didn't mean to pry. I followed your awards up the stairs. I'm fascinated by all of the memorabilia. It's like a dog museum in here." He waited, expecting her to throw him out, but she didn't seem angry with him for wandering around her home.

"Tea is ready."

He followed her back downstairs and she served him in the sitting room. Crowley half expected dog biscuits, but she offered custard creams with the tea, both of which were very good.

"Thank you," he said. "Excellent cup of tea!"

She didn't reply, sipped at her own cup.

Crowley pointed to the huge stuffed black dog in the armchair. "He isn't called Shuck, is he?"

"That story isn't true."

Crowley smiled, nodded. This woman was harder to converse with than the teenagers at the Academy. "I'll get to the point." Her nod was clearly relieved. "Some of our students snuck out of bounds last night. Just the usual teenage stuff, but they got quite a scare. They were chased by what they described as a huge black dog. One of them even said the dog had glowing eyes. They think it was Black Shuck."

"Black Shuck isn't real," Egerton said.

"No, of course, I understand that. But I wondered if you might know of someone who lives near the old church and might own a very large black dog? I saw some paw prints and they were huge. Twice the size of Jackie's prints out there." He nodded toward the window and the neat garden beyond.

"Not my dogs," Egerton said, glancing away. "My dogs are well trained, and always in at night."

"Oh, I believe you," Crowley said, though he still felt suspicious. "Have you heard tell of a dog this size in the area?"

A shudder seemed to pass over Egerton. "Look to the pub," she said, then pressed her thin lips together.

"Someone at the pub owns this dog?"

Egerton sipped her tea, wouldn't meet his eye. "Look to the pub."

It was clear the woman was getting agitated. "I'll do that, thank you. I appreciate your advice."

Egerton relaxed a little, but Crowley's instincts told him the woman had more to tell. He sipped his tea, trying to think of a way to get her to open up some more. He was sure there was more to learn from her.

"Eric was a student at Scarsdell," Egerton said suddenly.

Crowley was surprised, but grateful she'd finally offered something in the way of conversation. "Yes, I saw that in the photograph. He's a handsome young man."

"He died," she said emotionlessly. She stared through Crowley, maybe looking into some distant, less painful past.

He didn't know what to say. "I'm so sorry," he managed.

"On a Ludus Historia outing," she said, her gaze coming back to pierce Crowley.

He frowned. "I'm new to the staff, but I get the impression the school history club is controversial," he said.

She held his gaze, her eyes glittering with more focus than she'd shown previously. "Ludus Historia is evil," she whispered harshly. She immediately looked around, as if searching for unseen eavesdroppers.

Crowley nodded, sympathetic. He thought he might

feel similarly bitter about a club if his child had died on an outing.

"This is their sign." She made the sign of the horns, index finger and pinkie extended, thumb holding down the two middle fingers.

"Is it?" Crowley said, thinking any kid who liked hard rock or heavy metal might make that sign. But the horns gave him an idea. He took out his phone, held it up to show her the photo of the bull and sun mosaic he had seen underground. The one that had now mysteriously vanished. "Have you ever seen anything like that before?"

She leaned forward to see better, then gasped. Her eyes were more intense than ever. "Look... to... the... pub."

Crowley was taken aback by her intensity. "Does the black dog have something to do with this?"

She collapsed back in her chair, hugged herself, and shook her head.

"Is it something to do with the history club?"

She let out a low groan and said, "The pub." She hung her head, shoulders quivering.

"Ms. Egerton, should I call someone for help?"

Her head whipped up, mouth downturned. "Leave me alone!" she shouted, venom in her tone. A number of dogs began barking.

"I'm sorry I upset you, that certainly wasn't my intention."

"Please leave!"

He stood and moved to the hallway. Jackie stood right outside the still open front door, head low, eyes baleful. Crowley licked his lips, nervous.

"Jackie, away," Egerton said. There was no way she could see the dog from where she still sat. When Crowley looked back to the door, the large dark dog was gone.

He quickly left the cottage. Jackie was nowhere to be seen. As he closed the door behind himself, he heard Egerton say again in a low, mournful voice that chilled him to the bone, "Look to the pub."

12

Scarsdell Academy

When Crowley got back to Scarsdell Academy, he had a sensation of discomfort squirming in his gut. It was no surprise that, like every other village in England, Market Scarston had its secrets; age-old arguments and allegiances, that festered and grew well beyond their original bounds. He also knew that private schools bred contempt, both within their walls and certainly with the community in which they were located. But there seemed to be something more to events of the last couple of days. Nothing he could put his finger on, but the same sense that had saved his life in the Middle East tingled now. The same ephemeral trepidation that had made him pause behind a wall in a run-down, bombed-out village and given him a moment to spot the booby-trap that would otherwise have killed him and his entire squad ticked in his hindbrain now in this quiet, simple English village.

Pull yourself together, Jake, he told himself. Jumpy and scarred from bad experience. No need to get carried away by a crazy, lonely old woman who had lost her son. Then he remembered that she wasn't actually all that old. And she had lost her son in unusual circumstances. Alert but not alarmed, that was the way forward. He needed to talk to young Tommy Arundel again.

The boys all lived in dorms of four beds, and Davenport told Crowley that Tommy had retired to his. When Crowley reached Tommy's room, he found that the young man wasn't alone. Crowley immediately recognized the other man present from various photos around the school. Philip Arundel, Scarsdell Academy old boy, benefactor, and Tommy's father.

The man wasn't what Crowley would have expected,

despite the photos he'd seen. Philip was clearly a physically fit man, tall, and he moved with an air of vigor. His face bore that permanent sneer of faint disdain so common on people from old money English families, but he was handsome all the same. He had to be at least fifty years old, but aside from a few lines on his face and a touch of gray around the temples, he looked a decade younger. Father and son both turned as Crowley entered.

"How are you, Tommy?" Crowley asked.

"I'm okay, thanks, Sir." The young man managed a tight smile. His father couldn't be happy that he'd strayed out of bounds and gotten himself hurt.

"Philip Arundel." The man stepped between his son and Crowley, clearly annoyed that Crowley had addressed the boy first. Crowley allowed himself a little juvenile pleasure at the deliberate slight.

"Jake Crowley," he said, returning the handshake.

Arundel smiled, showing altogether too many teeth. "Thank you for rescuing my son," he said, his handshake a bit too firm, held a bit too long.

Crowley resisted the urge to squeeze back. He did hold on for a just a moment longer as Arundel finally went to pull his hand away. A flicker of annoyance rippled the man's eyebrows, but Crowley turned immediately to Tommy. "Still sore from the fall?"

"Not bad. I'm to remain off my feet for today. At least, that's what Nurse said."

"I understand you displayed some useful skills." Arundel looked at Crowley, arched an eyebrow. "Both in finding and initially treating Tommy."

"Just common sense really."

"Ah, come now, Mr. Crowley. No place for false modesty here. You've had field experience of some kind. I can tell simply by looking at you, let alone the things you did for my son."

Crowley smiled, dipped his head just slightly, but refused to answer. Arundel's brow knotted. It clearly rankled him that Crowley wasn't forthcoming, and Crowley enjoyed that. He was also cautious for more serious reasons. *Look to the pub*, Egerton had said. And Crowley couldn't help thinking *Look to the school* might be equally good advice. He had quickly come to suspect everyone around him, and self-important, old-money men like Philip Arundel would top the list of people Crowley would distrust regardless of the situation.

"Where's home for you then?" Arundel asked, taking a new tack. "Your accent isn't local."

"I don't really have a home other than here, now," Crowley said, with a half-smile. "I've moved around a lot previously."

"Oh? And where were you before this position?"

Crowley was in no doubt that the school's biggest benefactor had seen his CV. The truth was that Arundel probably already knew a lot more about Crowley than Crowley would like. But this was a question he couldn't politely skirt.

"I was in the service."

Arundel waited for more, head slightly tilted. When Crowley didn't elaborate, Tommy's father flashed a knowing smile. Despite his annoyance at Arundel winkling an admission from him, a sense of understanding passed between the two men. Crowley suspected he'd moved up a notch in Arundel's estimation. That in itself gave him an interesting insight into the man.

"What's your line of work?" Crowley asked.

"Shipping."

Now it was Crowley's turn to wait, and this time Arundel was not forthcoming. A silence hung between them, each taking the other's measure. Tommy looked from Crowley to his father and back again, brow slightly furrowed.

"I know the students are happy to have you here," Arundel finally said, filling the void that had been growing. "Tommy speaks very highly of you."

Crowley laughed. "Oh, I doubt that, but it's kind of you to say." Tommy showed little to no interest in class, no doubt relying on his family connections. He was one who would never have to actually work for anything in his life, other than work at fulfilling the obsequious role of son to a powerful father. As long as he remained in his father's good graces, life would be permanently on a silver platter for Tommy Arundel. Crowley himself enjoyed more privileges than the average person, but the sense of entitlement resident in families like the Arundel's made his skin crawl.

"I'm sure you didn't just come up here to check on the boy's injuries," Arundel said. "Don't let me interrupt you." He made a show of stepping back just a meter or so, then gestured generously toward his son.

Crowley saw no harm in telling the truth. He would watch the father's reaction too. "Remember the mosaic we saw in that underground chamber?" he asked. "I wanted to talk about it some more. I wondered why it seemed to upset you."

"Why would Tommy know anything about that?" Arundel snapped, suddenly defensive. He seemed personally affronted.

There's a glimpse of his true nature showing through, Crowley thought. "Well, because Tommy is both a local and a member of the history club," he said.

Arundel nodded. "Well, yes. The history club is a family tradition."

"Is that so?" Crowley pulled out his phone, showed Arundel the photo of the mosaic. "You ever seen anything like that before?"

Arundel leaned forward, took a long, hard look, then shook his head. "Fascinating, but nothing I'm familiar with." Crowley opened his mouth to ask more, but Arundel spoke on. "Did you know you are now a local celebrity, thanks to this find?"

"Celebrity? I hardly think that's likely."

"Oh, don't underestimate its significance, Mr. Crowley. The villagers believe the pit Tommy literally stumbled into is evidence that the battle of Blood Field happened right here in Market Scarston. It legitimizes our claim. One to our side, eh?"

"I've noticed the enmity between the two villages," Crowley said. "It seems a little extreme."

Arundel smiled, shook his head slightly. "It all started with the construction of a munitions plant in Wellisle during World War I. That village and ours were competing for the plant, and when it went to Wellisle, that turned the fortunes of both villages. Businesses grew up around the plant, people followed the jobs. The wealthier families even drifted that way." He looked up into memory, as if he'd been there. "Market Scarston was always the noble village, and Wellisle working class. Then, about ten years ago, the map was redrawn so that many of our local estates are suddenly located in Wellisle. It's apparently a more desirable address these days." He barked a rueful laugh, but Crowley saw the anger burning in his eyes. This was obviously very personal to him. "But we have the school," Arundel went on, pride replacing resentment in his tone. "Wellisle will never have a school with our history and traditions."

At the mention of the word history, Crowley seized the moment to bring the conversation back around. "I must admit, I know nothing about the history club."

"We study local history," Tommy said. "All the way back to the days of Roman rule."

"And before," Arundel added sharply.

Tommy nodded, chastised. "And before. We do a lot of outdoor activities, hiking, camping, even archaeological digs."

"It seems strange," Crowley said carefully, "that given I'm the geography and history teacher here that I have no involvement."

Arundel chuffed a condescending laugh. "Ah, despite its name, it's really more of a social and outdoorsman club than an actual history group."

"Speaking of the club," Tommy said. "I have an outing."

"I thought you were supposed to rest?" Crowley said

"That's what Nurse says," Tommy said. "But I'm

feeling quite well, actually." He headed for the door. "See you later, Dad, Sir."

Arundel watched his son leave, then turned back to Crowley. "You can't keep young people still for a moment."

"So it would seem."

Arundel reached out to shake hands again. "I do hope to see you again soon." There was no challenge to Arundel's grip, but it was firm, his gaze flinty.

"I look forward to it," Crowley said.

13

Crowley headed out into the school grounds, to walk and think. Scarsdell Academy lay in close to twenty acres of prime real estate, the wall on one side butting up to the forest, the long gravel driveway leading out to the main road into the village. In between the school building and the back wall were acres of well-manicured lawns, garden beds with perennials and flowers, several neatly trimmed bushes, and in the middle a large formal garden with almost maze-like box hedges and a variety of statuary. Most of it honored Rome and the Romans. Curvaceous women holding amphorae, Romulus and Remus as babes under the snarling protection of a wolf, Hercules capturing the Cretan Bull, Evander of Pallantium holding tablets as he brought the Greek pantheon, laws, and alphabet to Italy.

Crowley wandered among them all, pausing to look from time to time. He taught these myths and legends and more, and was fascinated by them. He couldn't help wondering where the mosaic he had seen underground might fit into the stories.

He rounded a tall corner of jade green and saw Emma sitting on one of the low marble benches, a book resting on her knee. She seemed to have forgotten it was there as she stared out into nowhere, lost in thought. She jumped as Crowley stepped into view.

"Sorry, Emma. Didn't meant to startle you."

"That's okay. I'm tired. Still haven't really caught up from the late night." She grinned sheepishly.

"How are you?" Crowley asked. "Other than tired."

Emma shrugged. "I'm fine, I guess."

"Still a little spooked?"

"Yeah. But perhaps we got it wrong?" She made the

suggestion into a question, like she wanted Crowley to reassure her.

He wanted to do just that, but had received different spooks of his own earlier in the day and felt discomforted. "Regardless," he said instead. "You're safe now."

"Yes, Sir." She stood, turned to leave.

"Hold on a moment, do you mind?"

She turned back to him, brow furrowed.

"What do you know about Ludus Historia?" he asked.

She frowned. "It's a boring club for the rich boys."

"Rich boys like Tommy?"

Emma nodded. "He and Chas mention the club all the time, but they never really say anything."

"What do you mean?"

She thought for a moment, then said, "Like, they'll share an inside joke and when we ask what they mean, they say 'the club', all mysterious, like it's a secret and we're not supposed to know. Then they flash that stupid sign." She made the heavy metal sign of the horns and Crowley frowned to see it again.

On a hunch, he sharply asked, "What do you all get up to at the Leaping Hound?"

"Nothing, really," Emma said reflexively, then turned beet red, realizing her admission.

"I found your beer cans in the church yard." Crowley lowered his voice. "Look, I'm not out to get any of you into trouble. But part of my job is to keep my students safe, and I take that very seriously." His heart raced, his mind dredging up old memories, mostly of failure. His old commanding officer yelling in his face, *You made that choice did you not, Crowley?*

Emma wilted beneath the intensity of his stare, mistaking his pain at the memory for anger at her and her friends. She looked around, then said, "To be honest, we rarely ever go *into* the pub. We have a friend in the village who gets us beer and cigs, but that's all. We don't cause any harm, Sir, I promise."

"Who did you meet from the village last night?"

Crowley asked. He remembered the two sets of footprints leading back to the lane, running the other way to the rest.

Emma shifted her feet, clearly uncomfortable.

"You can tell me," Crowley said. "I won't tell anyone else." He wondered who she was afraid of upsetting.

"I know we're not supposed to hang out with village kids," Emma said. "But Tommy has a girlfriend from there, and Nats is seeing one of the village lads."

"Right," Crowley said, gently, his tone leading her. He didn't really see the problem.

Emma swallowed. "I mean, no one minds about Nats, and her family is all cool, but if Tommy's dad knew he was going out with a village girl, he'd go ballistic."

Crowley nodded. There it was. For all his talk of this village being the best one, Philip Arundel didn't want his son running around with the common folk. "So, who's Tommy seeing?" he asked.

"Her name's Katie."

"Is she connected to the pub?"

Emma shrugged. "Nat's boyfriend, Marcus, gets us the beer. But Katie's lowlife brother hangs around The Leaping Hound all the time." She shifted again, clearly concerned she'd already said too much. Crowley still didn't quite understand her discomfort, but maybe it was as simple as rich family politics. Before he could ask more, Emma said, "I really have to go, Sir." She turned and hurried away.

Crowley strolled back towards the school, not really sure how much more he'd learned. He needed time to try to put the pieces together, but he wasn't certain any of the pieces he had would fit into a bigger picture.

He bumped into Beth Morgan, who narrowed her eyes when she saw him. "You look like you lost ten pounds and found a penny," she said.

"Walk with me a minute?"

As they walked across the lawns under the autumn sun, Crowley summarized the day's events, laying out all he'd seen and done. He finished with the conversation he'd just had with Emma and said, "What do you think?"

"I don't know what to think about any of it," Morgan said. "But I'll tell you what. You go and see what more you can find out about the pub. Egerton's words strike me as worth following up. In the meantime, leave the history club to me."

14

Rose Black decided to spend her Saturday afternoon outside the museum. She had done enough overtime, after all, especially considering it was unpaid.

She had plenty of time until her appointment, so she bought a coffee and went for a stroll through Kensington Gardens. The phone call from Elizabeth Morgan had piqued her interest like nothing else had in recent months. Rose had a feeling the discovery Morgan told her about might be quite important.

"What I could use right now is a professional archaeologist," she said aloud as she looked at the photographs of the odd subterranean chamber. "A real Indiana Jones type."

The Albert Memorial lay just ahead and she drifted in that direction. It was one of her favorites in London. Its tall, ornate canopy sheltered a gilded statue of Prince Albert. All around were works of art devoted to the arts, the sciences, industry, and to various parts of the world.

Near the Albert statue, a crowd had gathered around a tall man. Rose did a double-take. He was Native American, a rare sight in London. He was also tall, powerfully built, and ruggedly handsome.

As she continued to drift in that direction, the man got down on one knee in front of a blonde-haired woman. He was proposing! The sight brought a lump to Rose's throat. She blinked away tears.

"Don't be an idiot," she whispered. "You're so much better off."

As she drew closer, she made out what the man was saying.

"…have made my life worth living. And I have never

minded that you're transgendered," the man said. The woman's jaw dropped, her eyes went wide.

That was a bit personal, but good on him for not caring, Rose thought. And then a couple of things caught her eye. There was a ghost of a smile on the man's face. And another man, a blond fellow, was scaling the Albert statue.

"It's so romantic," a woman standing nearby whispered.

Rose rolled her eyes. The proposal was fake—a diversion. Must be some kind of prank. She shook her head and hurried away.

"What a couple of absolute morons."

From Kensington Garden, she caught an eastbound bus. After exhausting what research she could in the museum archives, Rose had been left with one clear route forward: Mithras.

Mithraism as a religion was, in itself, fascinating. One of the ancient mystery cults, details of its practices and worship were sketchy due to its nature as a secretive sect, but it predominantly involved the worship of the Persian god Mithras in caves. It flourished from the second through fourth centuries of the common era. Long before the Illuminati, the Masons, or the Templars had instituted their secret handshakes and mysterious brotherhoods, ancient Rome had its own secret societies. Romans worshipped Mithras as the god of the sun, along with a large pantheon of other deities. The male-only Cult of Mithras worshipped the god as a hero in a battle between good and evil. Garrisons all over the Roman empire had temples dedicated to Mithras, called Mithraeum. These were often underground, in reference to the legend of Mithras slaying a bull in a cave. All Mithraea featured a tauroctony, an image of the god Mithras slaying the sacred bull, as its centerpiece. This fit so neatly with the photographs of the mosaic Morgan had sent through that Rose couldn't imagine it being anything else. Especially as Morgan had said the mosaic was discovered in a recently unearthed underground chamber.

The covert religion of Mithraism was once so widespread some historians considered it an early rival to Christianity, even a sister religion. But due to the secrecy of its practice, little could actually be known for certain. No reputable written accounts of the religion had been found, and all the facts and conjecture were based on physical artifacts and dedicatory inscriptions from archaeological finds, along with more than a thousand pieces of sculpture.

Rose needed more details than these superficial histories, and there was one place in London she hoped she could get it—the reconstructed Temple of Mithras. The Mithraeum in Londinium had been built in the late second century, but seemed to have fallen out of use by the early fourth, matching her research of the religion's heyday. Built eighteen feet below street level to create a symbolic cave emulating the one where Mithras slew the bull, it was sealed up for centuries.

A statue of Mithras slaying the Astral Bull was found in 1889, but the temple itself was not unearthed until 1954, during the construction of a modern office development. Subsequent development in London's financial district lead to the Mithraeum being disassembled and rebuilt on Queen Victoria Street. In 2009 the Temple was removed, with the intention of relocating it in the new Walbrook Square development, back where it had originally been found. Long legal wrangling had prevented this, but the Temple had recently been reassembled not far from the site it originally occupied.

Rose got off near the Lord Mayor's mansion, and made her way on foot to the Mithraeum. From the outside it wasn't much to look at. Once inside, Rose revised her assessment. Behind glass walls, the ancient walls and stones of the once underground chamber were laid out exactly as they had been almost two thousand years before. A central channel led between two slightly raised areas to a half-circle chamber at one end. In this space was an engraved glass representation of the god slaying the bull, which in its day in Roman times would likely have been a mosaic. Several people wandered around the large space, looking into the ruins, reading the plaques describing the religion, its history, the discovery and relocation of the Mithraeum. But Rose knew all that. She needed more.

As she looked up and scanned the space for someone to talk to, a man caught her eye. He was wearing a neat shirt with a name badge, his gray hair slightly ruffled, balding on top. She guessed he was about sixty, with a slight rounding in the middle that made him jolly-looking with his wide smile and gentle eyes. He ruined the image entirely when he approached her and licked his lips.

"And what can I do for you, young lady?"

Rose's first thought was simply, *Ugh.* But despite an urge to kick him in the nuts, she'd hit a dead end in her research, and he was no doubt the expert in Mithraism. His name badge read *Mark Doncaster.*

"Mr. Doncaster, I wondered if I could ask some questions."

"Only if you promise to call me Mark." He actually winked at her.

She forced herself to laugh off her discomfort. "If you insist."

"And what's your name?"

"I'm Rose."

Doncaster looked her up and down, then gave his slimy smile again. "A very English name for a woman with a touch of the Orient in her blood?"

Rose drew a deep breath. "My mother is Chinese, my father is English." She didn't owe this man any explanations of her personal story, but if she could move past this awful interaction as quickly as possible, she could learn what she needed and get out.

"Well," he said. "Isn't that wonderful."

Time to move on, Rose thought. "I wondered if I could ask you a little about the religious practices of Mithraism?"

"Certainly."

She told him that she knew about the general history of the sect. She was convinced the old mosaic and the odd chamber Morgan had described were connected to Mithraism, but she was reluctant to give anything away about the discovery. At least, not yet. She asked if he could elaborate.

Doncaster slipped into his lecturer role and gave her some background on the Mithras Cult and the temple. It wasn't anything new to her, but she let him talk a little while. Then she asked, "But what did they actually do during their worship?"

Doncaster smiled. "You mean the ritual slaughter?"

There were two words that made Rose distinctly uncomfortable. "Sure," she said anyway.

"The taurobolium," Donacaster said. "The sacrifice of the bull, in deference to Mithras slaying the sacred bull. Some cosmologies suggest it was a slaying of the actual zodiac of Taurus, but that's been largely debunked. Mithraism was originally thought of as a 'star cult', with strong ties to astrology and astrotheology. But according to Ulansey, Mithras is actually Perseus, the Greek hero, and is hidden in a realm beyond the cosmos. Another thinker on the subject, Michael Speidel, suggest he's actually Orion. Roger Beck argues that we shouldn't read the tauroctony as a star map, as there probably isn't a constellation to match Mithras. Then there's Abolala Soudavar, one of the few minds to believe Mithraism actually has Persian roots. Regardless, most modern historians and archaeologists agree we're really no closer to revealing the cult's secrets with absolute finality than the Romans were millennia ago when they dubbed the cult the 'Mithraic Mysteries.' So, anything is entirely guesswork."

Doncaster grinned like this was all a huge joke, then he raised one finger when Rose drew breath to talk. "But!" he said. "We believe they bathed in the blood of the sacrificed bull, hence the trench there through the center, you see? The worshippers would stand in the trench, the bull would be led to the edge of the trench and its throat cut. In some cases, a strong grating was built over the trench so worshippers could stand directly underneath the bull as it was slaughtered."

Rose grimaced at the thought, but it was some powerful imagery all the same. "It sounds similar to Christianity, in a way," she said. "All that being 'bathed in the blood of the lamb.' Only a bull and rather more literal."

"It's a fairly common part of many ancient religions," Doncaster said with a nod. "Christianity started out as a works-based faith, but as it grew in popularity among the Romans, the beliefs and symbolism of ancient religions were absorbed into religious writings and practices. Change was constant. It's only really in recent centuries that these religions have become so dogmatic."

"Which is why, in the older gospels, Jesus sounds like a simple Hebrew teacher who wants people to take care of one another," Rose said. "Yet by the time the Gospel of John was written, he's talking like a Greek philosopher."

Doncaster laughed, but nodded again. "You're well-educated, young Rose. As you read the later writings of the New Testament, the influence of Paul and other Romans is clear. The baptism imagery, the tenet that asking for forgiveness is paramount–"

Sensing a lecture coming, along entirely tangential lines, Rose said, "I have something to show you." Doncaster paused, mouth still half open. He waggled his eyebrows but Rose chose to ignore that. She showed him some photos of the chamber that Morgan had sent to her earlier. "Could this be a taurobolium?"

Doncaster's eyes went wide. He looked around, as if suddenly expecting spies or enemies to be descending on them. "Where is this place?"

Rose made a wry face. "I'm not at liberty to say."

His expression hardened, so she quickly resorted to charm. Though she couldn't stand the creep, she needed to keep him on side. She had clearly caused him some discomfort with the image. "At least," she said, with a coy smile, "not where prying ears can hear."

Doncaster softened again. He smiled. "Come this way." He led her to his office, a small but immaculately neat space with a dark wood desk and a bookshelf in one corner. Two chairs sat facing the desk, which he indicated.

As Rose said, Doncaster turned to the shelves and took down an old-looking book. He sat at his desk and flipped through the book for a moment, then turned it to face her.

A photograph showed an excavated chamber very much like the one in the photo from Elizabeth Morgan. There was a similar deep, narrow trench running through the center of the chamber, but this one hadn't been filled with earth like the one Morgan had told her about.

"You think the one in my photo has been filled in with dirt and debris before the chamber was closed up?"

Doncaster nodded, closing the book again. "It seems likely, though I don't know why. Closed up, you say? So, the one in your photo is a recent discovery?"

Rose was annoyed she'd let that detail slip. "I can't really say right now."

Doncaster came around the desk and leaned against it right in front of her chair, much too close for comfort. "I thought you promised to tell me the location of the chamber, here in private?"

"One more question," she said, biting down her distaste. She showed him the photo of the mosaic. "Can you identify this?"

His eyes went even wider than before, then he said, "No, I've never seen anything quite like that one."

Rose knew he was lying, but had no idea why. What was she uncovering here? Despite the bile rising in her throat, she turned on more charm. She stood and ran his tie between her fingers. "I can tell you know something, Mark. What's the big secret?"

He trembled and Rose wondered how long it might have been since a woman flirted back with him, if ever. "You must tell me where this was found," Doncaster said, a little breathlessly. "It's critical."

She figured she had to give him something if she was to learn anything else. "A village in Suffolk. It was discovered accidentally by a boy from a local school there. I'm afraid that's all I know." She ran a finger over his tie again. "But you must know a little more about this, surely?"

Doncaster swallowed, but a frown creased his brow. "That mosaic, it was the symbol of a tiny sect of Mithraism called Tauro Solis. It was believed to have died out long before the Romans reached England. I have to say, if this is authentic, it's quite a find." His demeanor had changed. His ogling eyes were troubled and he shifted away from her personal space, suddenly business. "What village in Suffolk?" he pressed. "You must tell me all the details you have."

"I already told you all I know. I'm researching on behalf of someone else, called Elizabeth. I don't recall her surname," Rose lied. "I have her number, but it's back at my office."

"Can you please tell me? I'd really like to visit this place."

Rose almost preferred the flirtatious creep to this neediness. She felt a strong urge to leave. "I'll call you with it as soon as I get back to my office."

"What about you write it down and let me know over dinner?"

"Hmm, I don't think so." At his angry expression, she added, "I have a boyfriend." It galled her that men wouldn't respect a woman's boundaries unless she was the 'property' of another man, but right now, she really needed him to back off.

His expression tightened, probably realizing she'd been playing with him. He brought it on himself, after all. He forced a smile. "Can't blame a man for trying. I didn't catch your surname, Rose. Or where your office is?"

Rose backed to the door and pulled it open. "I'll call you with that number," she said, stepping back out into the open space of the reconstructed temple.

"You'll need my number," Doncaster said, opening a drawer.

Rose didn't wait for his business card or whatever else he might retrieve from his desk. She quickly closed his office door behind her and hurried out onto the street.

Doncaster stared at the closed door, grinding his teeth. He had admired her curves as she turned away, but he was annoyed she'd teased that bit of information out of him. He took a deep breath, then blew it out in exasperation. He was not looking forward to this.

"He's going to blame me. That's just how he is. Somehow, it will be my fault."

Trembling hands reached beneath his desk and stumbled for the tiny cylinder lock. Damn! The thing was bloody hard to work. He supposed it needed to be that way, else it would be hard to keep it a secret.

Secrets! He barked a rueful laugh.

"Oh, the secrets we keep," he whispered. He tried to force bravado into his words, but his voice quavered. He paused, closed his eyes and took two deep breaths.

"It's nothing he can't deal with. You're doing him a favor by forewarning him." A sudden sense of warmth filled him. Of course this could be buried. Probably literally!

He finally managed to enter his code and opened the hidden compartment built into his desk. He took out a small leatherbound journal, flipped to the back page and found, the phone number he needed.

He took another breath, let it out in a huff, and stood. He checked the number again then dialed it up on his desk phone. His heart raced as he listened to it ring. He half hoped it would go to voice mail. But after a moment, the call was answered.

"Yes?" came the curt reply on the other end. "What is it?"

"It's Mark Doncaster from the temple." Doncaster

took another breath, then said, "I think we have a problem."

15

Market Scarston

Crowley spent Saturday afternoon reading, trying to clear his mind of all the strange goings on. He trusted Morgan to find out what she could about the history society and there was little he could do in the meantime. As six o'clock rolled around he went down into the dining room and ate at the teacher's table, largely ignoring the students still around for the weekend. There were no other teachers there for that meal, even Morgan. As soon as he'd sated his hunger, he went back upstairs, got cleaned up and changed, then headed out.

As it was his job to check on the pub and see what he could learn there, he decided to walk. He'd never been a big drinker, but right now the thought of a few pints was quite enticing. And besides that, if he wanted to win the confidence of the locals, the best way was to drink with them. If he was truly a local celebrity, as Philip Arundel had condescendingly suggested, he might as well exploit it to gather some information.

It was long dark by the time he walked along the country lane from the school toward the village. High hedges on either side made the road narrow, but there was a kind of hard shoulder about a meter wide, marked with a solid white line of paint. Despite ensuring he stayed well inside it, he was only about half a mile along the lane when a screech of tires on the bend behind him made him leap sideways. He crashed into the hedgerow, which was thankfully forgiving enough to let him move out of the path of a small white panel van that barreled past. He didn't see the number plate or the driver. As he picked himself up and brushed leaves from his hair and jacket, he wondered if the driver was trying to harm him or if it was entirely accidental.

On the winding road he couldn't be certain the driver knew he was there. Regardless, whoever it was had been going much too fast for the narrow, twisty lane. Reckless at the very least.

Rattled, and suspicious the event had been deliberate, Crowley slipped off the road and into the forest as soon as the lane allowed. He made his way around to the village by a dog-legged route, creeping through the trees to spy on the pub without being seen walking past.

From the vantage point he gained he could see the front of the pub and its tables and benches, most occupied. The pub door was open, several patrons inside, drinking and chatting and laughing. Music drifted out, the jukebox playing the Rolling Stones. He could also see the car park beside the pub, and the extension to it where it went around behind the building, leading to the pub garden. The panel van that had almost hit him was parked there at the back.

Rupert Boles, the one who'd grabbed Morgan in their drunken attack, stood by the van chatting with another man, whom Crowley presumed to be the reckless driver. He wondered where Rupert's father was and whether another run-in with that man was imminent.

Staying in the shadows of the woods, Crowley watched Rupert and the other man talk for a minute or two more, then money was exchanged. Rupert looked around, presumably to ensure they were alone, then unlocked a cellar door at the foot of the back wall of the pub. He hurried down some steps, vanished for a moment, then returned with a small box stamped with the Tetley Tea logo.

Crowley frowned. Was the kid selling the bar's supplies right out the back of the pub? And how did he have access to those places? Crowley thought perhaps he needed to figure out just how Rupert and his father were connected to the Leaping Hound. And if whatever Rupert had just handed over were supplies from the pub, surely they'd be stored inside. So perhaps the small box contained something else entirely. But what? Perhaps this external basement was old and not used by the publican any more.

More questions.

The reckless driver had a few more words with Rupert, then got back in the van and drove away. Rupert looked around again then double checked the basement door was locked. He pocketed his keys and walked back around to the front of the pub and went inside.

Crowley pursed his lips. On the one hand, he wanted to go in and chat to the locals, see what he could learn. In particular, he wanted to figure out who Rupert and his father really were. But he also thought perhaps he was right in that Rupert used the old cellar without the knowledge of the publican. In which case, it would be a good idea to check it out while he knew Rupert himself was busy inside the Leaping Hound.

In the deep shadows of the early autumn night, Crowley moved along the tree line, then hurried across the road and came up to the pub car park from the far side. He quickly slipped past a few parked cars to crouch in darkness by the old basement door. It was built at an angle up against the pub wall, but the ground around it showed little wear and tear. If beer barrels were frequently rolled this way, that would have been evident.

The doors were wooden and closed with a simple hasp. That in turn had an old-fashioned padlock for security. Not worth much, Crowley thought with a smile. He'd picked up a few useful skills in the service and even more in the short and nefarious period since. Modern locks might be a little beyond his skill set, but old clunky arrangements like this were no challenge. He pulled his all-purpose pocket tool from his jacket and in moments had the padlock undone.

Wooden steps led down into darkness. Crowley flicked on his flashlight and descended, quietly closing the basement door above himself. The cellar was an old, musty space, with rickety wooden shelves around the walls, a bunch of wooden shipping chests, most open and empty, a few cardboard boxes. It was all just junk. A doorway in the far wall would have led in under the pub, but that had been bricked up. The bricks were a different size and color to the basement walls, so that confirmed Crowley's suspicion that this basement and the pub were no longer used together.

He saw a line in the dusty floor, footprints scuffing back and forth between the steps and the far corner. He followed them and found, hidden by loose burlap sacks, a very old cast iron safe. A quick inspection showed it to be solid and anchored in place. This, presumably, was where the tea was kept, in those small Tetley boxes. But he didn't think for a moment it was actually tea inside. A surreptitious night-time car park trade in tea bags seemed rather unlikely. So what was it?

He jumped at a scraping and knocking sound from behind. He quickly ducked into deep shadow behind a nearby shelf. Something on the floor on the far side of the basement shifted, then a hidden trapdoor in the floor opened up. A man climbed out, carrying a bag. He was tall and strong looking, though not bulky. He had a square-jawed face and short blond hair, shot through with the beginnings of gray. Crowley guessed him to be around fifty or so, but fit and vibrant with it. Crowley held his breath as the man pulled out a large key, opened the safe, and took out an envelope. He stood and counted the money inside by torchlight, then took out a few bills and pocketed them. Then he tucked the envelope with the rest of the money still inside into his jacket.

He had a bag with him, which he sat on the floor and removed several boxes of Tetley Tea and put them into safe. He locked up the safe again and climbed back down the hidden trapdoor, closing it quietly behind himself.

Crowley stared for some moments, wondering just what the hell was going on here. Without any other obvious course of action, he gave it a few minutes, then cautiously followed the stranger.

16

Market Scarston

As he lowered the old trapdoor as quietly as possible, Crowley heard scratches and scrapes from up ahead. He sat on the splintered wooden steps and waited. Patience was the key. He needed to know more without being seen. The sounds faded and Crowley sat in silent pitch darkness for another few minutes, just to be sure. Hearing nothing more, he cautiously moved down the steps, running the fingertips of his left hand along the rough stone wall to keep his orientation.

When his knee jarred slightly at solid ground instead of another step, he knew he'd reached the bottom. He'd only descended about a dozen feet, but the air was cool and dry. He smelled dust and something else, a vaguely animal scent he couldn't place. He flicked on his small pocket flashlight and moved carefully along. By the soft light Crowley recognized the tunnel. While not the same one, it was the same style and design as those he'd followed before that had led him into the pub basement. And then only because of the crack in the wall, maybe the result of decades of land settling. His chest and lower back still smarted a little from the grazes he'd acquired there. It seemed Market Scarston had a labyrinthine network of old underground passages. After some hundred yards it came to a T-junction. Crowley looked left and right, uncertain.

Then a dim glow appeared up ahead to the left, along with more sounds of footsteps and shifting items. They sounded large, maybe boxes or crates. The man he followed had no reason for stealth and was busily working on something up there. Crowley crept forward, hoping for a better look. He heard a loud clang, then a sharp click, like a lock engaging, then everything fell into darkness but for his torch. Moving more quickly, Crowley sneaked forward only to find himself at an iron door. The passage was wide and high, and dark again since the door closed. Crowley saw it had an old lock and would be easy to pick. As he reached for his tool, a low growl filled the air.

Crowley's guts froze. The sound triggered something primeval in him. He turned slowly to see a red and glowing blur fly through the air, aiming for his head. He reacted purely on instinct, dropped and rolled forward to pass under whatever was jumping him. The thing felt massive as it passed over him and crashed into the door. In the hectic light of Crowley's dancing torch, he saw it land and whip around, the growl louder now, and guttural.

Crowley steadied his flashlight, backing away. It was a massive black dog, the biggest he had ever seen. His old aunt had once had a Saint Bernard, before she'd moved to America. That had been a big dog, though gentle and fun. This thing had to be half again the size of Aunt Gertie's pet.

And it was glowing a dull red, casting a soft, bloody radiance around itself. Crowley frowned, wondering what on earth could cause that. He saw what appeared to be a kind of powder scattered through the dog's fur. Had it been dusted with something to make it glow red? The dog growled, tensed to spring, lowering its front legs, bunching up its back. In the narrow confines of the tunnel, Crowley knew he wouldn't stand a chance. He'd been lucky to duck its initial attack, but it wouldn't miss again and there was no way he would be able to outrun it. But it crouched there, teeth bared, growling, and not attacking.

Crowley's whole body shook in fear, but he forced himself to draw a long, deep, steadying breath. "Easy, boy," he said in a soft, conciliatory voice. Hunched down in front of the door, the dog continued to growl.

Crowley frowned, remembering Tommy Arundel's story. The dog had chased the students, but hadn't harmed them. For all their fear, if it had meant to attack them, it would have. They could no more outrun this beast than he could.

"Maybe you don't want to hurt me, eh?" Crowley said, his voice friendly. "You just want to keep me away from the door, yeah?"

He took a single, tentative step back, hands raised, palms out at waist level. His heart hammered. The dog continued to growl, but didn't move. He took another step.

Fluorescent light flickered into life on the other side of the door, and Crowley realized there was a glass panel in the top center that he hadn't seen before as the room beyond was dark. And now he saw what the dog was protecting.

Rows and rows of white plastic tubes, each maybe a foot in diameter, raised a couple of feet off the ground. Evenly spaced along the tubes were round holes and in each round hole stood a vibrant green plant, with pointed, five-fingered leaves. Banks of lights hung over the crop, brighter than daylight, flooding out through the small glass window to illuminate the dog's broad, shaggy back and Crowley himself.

A massive, hidden marijuana farm. A hydroponic operation of some impressive scale. No wonder they wanted to keep people out.

Before whoever had turned on the lights had a chance to look out through the door and spot him, Crowley took another step back. Then another. He saw the large blond man moving between the rows of plants. He took two more steps, more urgently now, but keeping his eyes on the dog. The huge beast sat in silence, finally no longer growling, but it watched him intently.

"Hey, dog!" the blond man called, looking between the rows of plants. "Where the bloody hell are you?" He looked up towards the door. "Shucky! You didn't get out again, did you?"

The dog answered with a single, high yip, incongruous from such a large animal.

The man turned and headed straight for the door. The dog turned to look, and Crowley slipped quickly away, back along the tunnel toward the old trapdoor. He felt as though the answers were starting to fall into place. Some of them, anyway. He also had some new questions.

As he headed back toward the first tunnel, he spotted something on the wall of the T-junction that he hadn't noticed before. Some faint marks in the old, Roman stone. He shined his torch on it and leaned in for a closer look. It was old and worn, but clearly a carving in the shape of the bull and sunburst, similar to the design he'd seen in the mosaic. Puzzled, feeling a little too confused and dusty from his excursion to head into the pub after all, Crowley made his way back above ground and headed back to the school.

17

Rose Black made the most of her Sunday morning, enjoying a lie in and then a lazy breakfast. As she made a second coffee and felt awake enough to converse with strangers, she gathered her notes together and sat on the couch with her phone. A photo of herself and Lily on the mantlepiece caught her eye. She looked away. No point in spoiling an otherwise pleasant Sunday with thoughts of her sister right now.

She dialed the number Elizabeth Morgan had given her. It rang a few times, then, "Hello, this is Elizabeth Morgan."

"Hi, it's Rose Black. From the museum?"

"Yes, hi. How are you?" She sounded surprised that Rose had called her back.

"I'm well, and I've got some interesting stuff to tell you."

"That's great, but hold on just a second."

Rose heard a muffled sound as Elizabeth seemed to cover the phone and then move from one place to another. There was a moment of background noise, lots of voices, as if Morgan was passing through a crowded room, then the clunk of a heavy door closing and silence.

"That's better," Morgan said over the line. "A bit of peace and quiet so I can concentrate."

"Busy there even on a Sunday morning?" Rose asked.

"Most of our students are boarders, and the majority tend to stay most weekends too. It's always busy here. Thankfully there's an office or two where the kids aren't allowed, and that's a sanctuary of sorts. A moment to hear yourself think. So, what have you learned?"

Rose pursed her lips, wondered how much she needed to warn Morgan. She decided full disclosure was her best option and let the woman, and the school, make their own decisions on how they moved forward. "I was up pretty late last night," she said. "I did some preliminary research, then managed to talk to an expert." She shuddered at the memory of Mark Doncaster. "That led me into a rabbit hole of research that turned up some fascinating details. First off, though, I think I should warn you."

"Warn me?" Morgan said. "Sounds ominous."

"Well, it's just that what you've uncovered there, if it's authentic, could be incredibly rare and really quite an archeological gem. I think you'll have all sorts of people wanting to get in on it if the details get out."

"Okay, thanks. I'll be sure to pass that on. Hopefully we can keep most of it under our hats at least for the time being."

Rose turned to her notes. "Okay, here's what I've learned. You seem to have uncovered a Taurobolium. I'll explain more about that in a second. But the chamber itself, with the trench through the middle, is a ritual chamber of Mithraism." Rose gave a cursory account of the general tenets and shape of the known history of the Cult of Mithras. "I'm sure you can easily look up more about that on your own," she said. "But this is where it gets interesting. The mosaic you sent me photos of, and the other descriptions you gave me, led me to learn that what you seem to have there isn't simply a Mithraeum, but a more specific and secretive sect even within the secret sect of Mithraism itself. Your chamber is a Mithraeum of Tauro Solis." She spelled it out and heard Morgan's pen scratching on notepaper. "Now, the Tauro Solis sect were particularly violent and bloodthirsty. In most Mithraeum, the worshippers would stand in the trench and bathe in the blood of a sacrificial bull. Your trench seems to have been filled in, either by accident or on purpose, maybe we can never know. But, your sect, the Tauro Solis, not only bathed in the blood of sacrificial bulls, they were into human sacrifice as well."

"My God, really?" Morgan's pen seemed to have

stopped moving.

Rose hoped the woman wouldn't forget to take notes. She pressed on regardless. "Yes, I'm afraid so. The Tauro Solis, while worshipping Mithras and sacrificing bulls, also centered their faith strongly around gladiatorial combat, animal sacrifice, and human sacrifice. So while they may have stood in the trench to receive a bull's blood, they may also have bathed in human blood. Many of their decisions were made through combat, almost always to the death but with that whole Caesar thing with the thumb up or thumb down, you know that?"

"Yes."

"Well, that was part of it too, apparently. Some sect members might lose in combat and be spared, others might be sacrificed. But on their most holy days, they would sacrifice a young man. Often an important one."

"This is really quite disturbing," Morgan said. "Do you know what days were the most holy to them?"

Rose smiled, turning the page on the couch cushion beside her knee. "Actually, I do. And it's quite timely to be discussing this now. The crazy thing is, tonight would be one of their most sacred nights. It's the autumnal equinox today. The equinoxes are the two days of the year when Tauro Solis celebrates the Sacrifice of the Son, their most powerful rite."

"So today is like their Easter," Morgan said, a nervous smile evident in her voice.

Rose laughed. "Not really, I'm afraid. In this ritual, they always sacrificed a young man, and the more noble the person sacrificed, the greater the honor. For both the one on the altar and the sect as a whole. But here's the really awful thing. If a father sacrificed his first-born son on this night, he was guaranteed eternal life. Now, I know these old school religions could be harsh and vicious, but that's really messed up, don't you think? What kind of man would sacrifice his own son for such selfish reasons?"

The humor in Morgan's voice drained away. "Let's not pretend there aren't some truly awful people out there, Miss

Black. Husbands and fathers throughout history have done far worse."

"I suppose you're right." Rose frowned at the sudden decline in Morgan's mood. "Are you okay?"

"Yes, thank you." Morgan was forcing a better demeanor now, but she sounded troubled. "I can't thank you enough for your help with this. I'll be sure to pass it all on."

"You're welcome. And please keep us in the loop? I have a colleague who would be desperate to see your site and learn more if he can."

"Of course, I won't forget your assistance. Thanks again."

Without waiting for an answer, the woman hung up. Rose stared at the phone for a moment. She wasn't offended by Morgan's curt farewell, but it bothered her that the woman seemed a little upset by it all. Maybe it was as simple as the gruesome practices of Tauro Solis. She shrugged it off, then caught sight of the photo of herself and Lily again. Morgan and her school would have to deal with it and be all right. Rose had problems of her own.

18

Scarsdell Academy

Crowley's biceps burned and sweat rolled down his face, but he pushed out another set. Physical exhaustion was the only thing he'd found so far that kept the nightmares at bay. The Army psychologist had assured him the symptoms would ease with time, as long as Crowley employed the various coping mechanisms they'd put in place. Plenty of exercise was the one that seemed to work best for him. And it kept him fit and strong.

He'd woken early, disturbed by bad dreams where village life in Market Scarston, incursions in Afghanistan, his youth and his misspent intervening years, all blurred into a carnival of darkness and confusion. A good night's sleep was a rare thing for him, usually broken at some point. He often startled awake in the small hours, blanketed by darkness and disorientation, not sure where he was or what had roused him, but a thin sheen of sweat would cover his skin. Other times, like today, dreams would tear him from rest as dawn smudged the sky and he knew there would be no further slumber.

Being a Sunday with no teacher duties requiring his attention, he'd started with a long run, then a small breakfast, then he hit the school's well-equipped gym. As he turned and lay back on the leg press, his phone buzzed on the floor beside him. He leaned over and looked down. A message from Morgan: *You up?*

Only for the last four hours, he thought. Instead, he texted back, *Yep*

Meet me in the staff lounge?

He pulled himself off the machine, told her he needed to shower and change and that he would be there in fifteen minutes. He hoped she had something interesting to tell him. He certainly had some news for her.

"Did I get you out of bed?" Morgan asked.

Crowley laughed. "No, I was in the gym. Been up a while." He made himself a coffee and sat across the small table from her. They were the only ones in the opulent staff rest area. Couches and armchairs filled one end, the other a selection of round tables, each with four chairs. Tea and coffee facilities, a microwave, and two large fridges filled one end wall.

"What have you learned about the history club?" Crowley asked.

Morgan frowned, shook her head. "I've done plenty of asking around but nobody wants to talk about it."

"You seem offended by that."

Morgan shrugged. "It's frustrating, that's all. I thought that, as a local myself, the students might be more likely to open up to me." She shook her head again. "Rich snobs," she muttered under her breath, but Crowley caught it.

"So, you're a village girl?" he asked her.

"We moved to London when I was ten, but I suppose I'll always be the mechanic's daughter."

"Nothing wrong with that."

She smiled. "Anyway, from what I gather, the history club is boys-only. Mostly from the well-off families, but they admit a handful of the best and brightest from among the rest of the riffraff. And you know what else? I get the impression there's an elite club, a sort of higher group within the wider club. Only a handful of boys are part of it and it seems that the likely members are all from only the richest and most well-established Market Scarston families."

Crowley nodded, thinking. "Tommy Arundel is a member, and his father Philip seems to be involved, and apparently an ardent supporter of all the club activities."

"That's not a surprise," Morgan said with a sigh. "Arundel is passionate about Market Scarston, and his influence on the school likely includes the history club. He's probably been in it since he was a student here. But what they get up to is shrouded in mystery. It could be nonsense and they keep secrets just for the sake of it. You know, to feel big and special. Or there could be more to it. I just can't find out."

"Talking of finding things out," Crowley said. "I discovered something quite interesting myself last night. Market Scarston has a significant hydroponic weed farm operating, literally under our noses."

"Seriously?" Morgan's eyes were wide in surprise. "Where?"

Crowley summarized his exploits of the previous day, including the presence of the huge dog, and its strange but artificial red glow.

Morgan sat back, shaking her head. She drained the last of her coffee. "Are you going to call the police about the marijuana operation?"

"To be honest I'm not all that fussed about someone making a living selling weed. There are far worse things in the world, and it's not something I really want to get tangled up in if I can avoid it."

"I suppose so." Morgan frowned. "But you look like something's bothering you."

"I'm thinking about my conversation with Egerton. She's a lonely and disturbed woman, but she was deadly serious about the pub. She kept insisting it was the center of everything. But the center of what?"

"Well, the dog is playing on the Black Shuck legends, and being used to keep people away from the weed," Morgan said "And it seems that weed is apparently being sold out of the pub. Or from the abandoned basement behind the pub anyway. People probably chat inside and that's where contacts are made for the deals."

Crowley nodded, though his brow was still furrowed. "Sure, that's definitely part of it. Could her son's death have something to do with that? It seems unlikely. But I wonder if there isn't more going on. When I showed Egerton the bull and sunburst design, she became upset, and again she pointed me to the pub. That's not related to the weed, I don't think. But I don't know what it is related to. It just feels like there's more to this. I feel like we're on the edge of discovering… something." He blew out a frustrated breath. "I can't pin it down." Then he remembered something else. "And what about the mosaic? Who wanted that gone and why? Someone tried to hide what small amount we discovered in that chamber."

Morgan pursed her lips in thought, then, "Maybe there was a passageway behind it that led to the marijuana operation. Perhaps they weren't hiding the mosaic, they just took it away in order to collapse the tunnel behind it so anyone investigating the taurobolium wouldn't discover the weed."

Crowley nodded, sat back. "That's a possibility. Actually, given the general location of things, that's quite likely. But we still don't know more about the activities of the history club and I feel like that's definitely worth investigating. Taurobolium, eh? Interesting."

"You know what that is?"

"It's my subject, sure. Cult of Mithras, sacrificial bulls, and so on. Is that what you learned? You think that's what the chamber is? I don't know much more than that, though."

"It's more than that, actually. I talked to a very nice woman at the Natural History Museum in London and she did some research for me. Turns out, according to her, that the chamber we discovered is indeed an old Cult of Mithras temple, but more than that it's from a very rare sect of Mithraism called the Tauro Solis."

"Is that right? Now that's something I haven't heard of before."

Morgan nodded, smiling. "Me either. It's pretty fascinating. And, according to the nice museum lady, this could potentially be an exciting find. Historians thought the sect had no presence in England after the Roman occupation, but this would indicate otherwise."

Crowley scratched his chin, thinking. "Could it have been someone from Wellisle who destroyed the mosaic?" he mused. "The discovery would be a feather in Market

Scarston's cap, after all. If anyone from Wellisle thought it might raise their rival village's standing, they might have tried to sabotage that."

"It's possible, I suppose."

"Oh, and I just remembered something else! When I followed that guy last night and discovered the hydro farm, I passed another bull engraving in one of the old passageways, between the pub and the growing operation. Do we have a map of the village?"

Morgan went to a bookcase and pulled down a tourist guide to the area. She thumbed through for a moment, then brought it back to the table. "Here. Not super detailed, but it looks roughly to scale to my eye."

Crowley traced a line with his fingertip, from the back of the pub, trying to estimate how far he'd travelled underground. "I think I found the bull symbol about here," he said, tapping the page. "And look how close that is to the old taurobolium young Tommy accidentally discovered. And the weed farm is here."

"Hmm." Morgan reached over and pointed to an area just to the north of the taurobolium site. "I'd never realized before, but look how close it all is to this particular property line."

"What's the relevance of that?" Crowley asked.

Morgan smiled. Crowley liked it when she smiled. "That's the Arundel estate. Maybe it means nothing, but maybe it's relevant?"

Crowley sat back and looked up at his colleague. "At the very least," he said, "I think we should have a talk with Tommy."

19

It was almost lunchtime when Crowley and Morgan went upstairs to the boys' dorm level. Crowley was pleased Morgan seemed to be softening toward him, opening up a little bit. He still sensed a little discomfort between them, she was guarded to some degree, but not as cold as previously. Then again, he hadn't called her Morgan for a while.

"Why don't you like being called Beth?" he asked before he could stop himself.

She glared at him as they mounted the last flight of steps and he wondered if he'd undone all that good will he was just thinking about. Then her eyes softened. "It's not so much that I don't like the name, only that it's what someone used to call me and that someone isn't around anymore. It makes me sad."

Crowley felt a wave of contrition. "Ah. That sucks, I'm sorry."

"It's okay. But I would prefer Elizabeth."

He nodded. "I'll try to remember." And he meant it. "Here we are."

He rapped on the door of Tommy's dorm, waited a polite couple of seconds, then opened it. There had been no reply and the room was neat, but empty. All the beds made, belongings tidied up as school policy dictated, but no one present.

"Annoying," she said.

The door across the hall opened and Crowley turned to see Bradley Davenport. He was the student who had woken Crowley on Friday night when Tommy didn't come back, and he was also the monitor for this floor. "Tommy isn't here," Bradley said.

"I can see that, son. Where is he? Any idea?"

"I don't know, Sir. I haven't seen him since yesterday afternoon."

"Since the history club meeting, you mean?"

Bradley looked away, his cheeks coloring slightly.

"Well?" Crowley said, hardening his voice slightly. "You going to answer me?"

"Sir, Tommy didn't show up for the outing."

Crowley noticed the young man had fresh bruises on his arms and an abrasion on his cheek. "What did you all get up to on the outing?"

"Oh, some hiking and climbing," Bradley said vaguely. "The usual kind of stuff, I guess."

"You're the hall monitor," Crowley said, changing tack. "Why didn't you report you had a student missing?"

Bradley shrugged. "I'm not worried about Tommy. He comes and goes a bit."

Special privileges in action, Crowley thought.

"You figured he was just out late with his village girlfriend?" Morgan asked.

"How do you know ab—" Bradley checked himself, but it was too late.

"We're not stupid," Morgan said with disdain. "And you lot are not as clever as you think you are. We know most of what goes on around here."

It was good to convince Bradley of that, Crowley thought, but they certainly didn't know much about the history club and that was beginning to bother him more and more. He made the sign of the horns, right up in front of Bradley's face. "What does this have to do with the history club?"

"Not the whole club." Bradley pressed his lips together, suddenly looking like he thought he'd said too much.

Crowley decided he'd had enough. He knew how to intimidate people, knew how to make himself a genuine threat. He brought some of his skills to bear, broadening his posture, lowering his tone of voice as he made hard eye contact with Bradley and moved into the boy's personal space. Bradley flinched, then seemed to wilt.

"Listen carefully," Crowley growled, "because this is the only chance I'll give you. Your family might be well-connected in Suffolk, but I promise you it's nothing compared to my connections." Tears balanced on the lower lids of Bradley's eyes and he pressed back against the wall. Crowley wasn't about to feel sorry for him though. The air of mystery that had surrounded Crowley since he arrived would pay dividends here. "I know how your family makes its money." That was a lie, but of course, Bradley was none the wiser. "And I can make sure the tax man traces every penny back to its source." An even bigger lie. Crowley had moved almost nose-to-nose with the boy. From the corner of his eye he saw Morgan looking both afraid and slightly impressed. He liked that. But he kept up the pressure on Bradley. "And that's nothing compared to what I'm trained to do."

Bradley's eyes were like saucers. "Sir, I–"

"Now, stop bullshitting me and tell me what I want to know!"

The boy looked around, trembling. His lower lip quivered and his voice was a whisper. "That sign is only to be used by a select few in the club." He swallowed, looked around again. "Arundel's favorites."

"Philip Arundel? Tommy's father?"

"Yes."

"And what's the deal with this select few?"

"I don't know, I swear. They never tell the uninitiated. All I know is the people who make it into Arundel's circle are taken care of even after they leave the school. It's a very big deal to be chosen. And if you upset Mr. Arundel, you'll never get in."

Bradley looked as though he thought his own chances were plummeting right now, thanks to this conversation. Crowley thought he was probably doing the boy a favor on that front. "What else?" Crowley asked.

Bradley shook his head, licked his lips. "I don't know. Oh, there's a special meeting tonight. Tommy let it slip yesterday. He was upset, and when he decided to skip the club meeting and outing, he mentioned that he wouldn't be participating in... what did he call it..?"

"Anything to do with the Vernal Equinox?" Morgan asked.

Bradley brightened. "That's it. 'I'm not going today and I'm not doing the Equinox either', that's what he said. I asked what he meant and he clammed up and said for me to forget about it."

Crowley and Morgan exchanged a knowing glance. "What's the connection between the history club and the ancient Roman mystery cults?" Crowley asked. Now the boy was talking, he needed to get as much out of him as possible.

Bradley appeared puzzled. "We honor our Roman heritage, that's the, you know, the genesis, of the club. And Mr. Arundel teaches us gladiatorial combat sometimes, but that's all."

"Is that how you got the bruises?"

Bradley nodded. "Mr. Arundel teaches us sword, spear, trident, hand-to-hand, all kinds of stuff. He's a real expert. He fights us four and five at a time sometimes, and we hardly ever lay a finger on him. We use blunted swords and plenty of padding, of course, but we still get pretty knocked around."

"You enjoy it?"

Bradley twisted his lips. "Sort of, I guess? It's not really my thing, but it is a thrill sometimes. Some of the boys love it though. And Mr. Arundel, he comes alive when he spars. You'd never think it, but he's so passionate about it."

"So what was Tommy upset about?" Morgan asked. "Why did he decide not to do all that stuff you mentioned?"

Bradley shrugged. "Like I said, he told me to forget about it, so I don't really know. But I get the impression Tommy's tired of being in the club, that's all. And of course, that causes friction with his dad. Sort of like the football coach's son quitting the squad, you know? But that's just my guess, I don't really know for sure."

"Where's this Equinox meeting being held tonight?"

Morgan asked.

"I don't know. I'm not in Mr. Arundel's circle, I'm not even supposed to know it's happening. Tommy could get into trouble for mentioning it at all."

"Have you heard of Tauro Solis?" Crowley asked.

Bradley's brow furrowed. "No. I don't know what that is."

He seemed sincere, his confusion genuine. Crowley nodded. "You are to inform me if you think of anything else, do you understand?"

"Yes, Sir."

"And you tell me immediately if you see Tommy or get word about where he is."

"Yes, Sir. I will."

Crowley leaned forward again, menacing. "I mean it, Davenport. Do not play games with me."

Bradley's face paled again. "No, Sir. I promise."

"Good. Off you go."

Bradley vanished into his dorm in a flash, closing the door behind him. Crowley and Morgan headed back for the stairs.

"Are you really as well-connected as all that?" she asked, her lips quirked in a slight smile.

Crowley just grinned.

Morgan shook her head, but the smile remained. "So where are we going now?"

"I want to check out the history club's meeting room."

20

Scarsdell Academy

As they walked back through the Academy, Morgan stopped into the admin office and found Tommy's home number. She rang, but no one answered. Then, on a hunch, she tried the Leaping Hound, but the publican told her he hadn't seen Philip Arundel or Tommy for a few days.

"We're running out of leads," she said, as she hung up.

"The club then," Crowley said.

The room set aside for history club activities was one of the larger spaces on the ground floor. Most of the similar sized rooms were classrooms, so it seemed to echo the general privilege of the club that they had such a prestigious piece of academy real estate. Crowley mentioned this to Morgan and she sneered.

"Nothing like a class system within a class system, eh?" she said.

"You're not keen on the wealthy elite," Crowley said, feeling slightly uncomfortable, though he was no blueblood. "Moreso than most, I mean."

Morgan shrugged. "I have no issue with wealthy people, per se. Some have worked hard and earned it, after all. Even some who have been born into money are decent people, down to earth and generous." That made Crowley feel slightly better. "But," she went on. "The kind who use their money to stand over regular people, or the kind who think their wealth is somehow proof of superiority? That galls me. Most family money is off the back of corruption or oppression or straight up crime. It might have been so long ago that you can't hold the current generation responsible for the sins of the fathers and grandfathers, but it doesn't make them better than anyone else. It just makes them lucky. The good fortune to be born into wealth. If anything it should be a trigger to do all they can for others, but instead they grow up with a sense of entitlement and elitism that only propagates more of the same. Arundel is a prime example of that and this club is almost an embodiment of the attitude. Sticks in my craw. Part of why I took this job is to try to deconstruct that attitude in the students."

"Fight the system from the inside, eh?"

"Exactly."

Crowley nodded, entirely understanding. A lot of his colleagues in the service and several associates since would qualify as working class or poor, often without options, without chances. It was indeed galling to see people with money think those others were somehow lesser when it all came down to good luck. Morgan made good points, eloquently. He resolved to find a way to offer some generosity beyond his personal circumstances, but for the moment he needed to concentrate on the task at hand.

The heavy, dark wooden door of the club had a fancy carved sign hanging on it: *Ludus Historia* in a curving, calligraphic script. He tried the handle but it was locked. Like others he'd seen, however, the lock was old and no match for his less respectable skillset.

"Maybe keep an eye on the corridor a moment?" he said.

Morgan frowned, but did as he asked, casting glances down as he worked. It only took moments and the lock popped. He opened the door and gestured for her to enter.

"You are full of surprises, Mr. Crowley."

He smiled. "I have all manner of talents. Honestly, though, their level of security is suspicious, no?"

"Perhaps, or perhaps not," Morgan said. "There are a lot of artifacts here."

There was a long dining table through the center of the room, a dark wood, maybe mahogany, with high-backed chairs all around it. Each chair had a striped gold and blue silk seat covering. The wood-paneled walls were hung with numerous paintings depicting gladiatorial combat of all kinds. Swordplay was prevalent, but other types of contest were present, even chariot racing. Standing around all the walls were display cases, glass-fronted, containing a wide variety of Roman artifacts.

Lots of old framed photos were on the walls too, or on the tops of the display cases. One large section of wall was reserved for club group photos, one for every year. There were dozens of them. Moving in for a closer look, Crowley saw that here and there a face and name had been blacked out.

In a photograph dated 1981, he recognized a very young Philip Arundel. After a moment he realized the familiar young man beside Arundel was Archie Beckett, the current Headmaster. And on Arundel's other side was another familiar-looking man, but Crowley couldn't place why he recognized the strong-jawed fellow.

Morgan moved beside him to see what he was paying such close attention to.

"Arundel and Beckett," Crowley said, pointing. "But who's that?"

"That's a young Kray," she said. "Robert Kray. He's considered something of a local thug but he mostly keeps to himself. I had no idea he'd gone to school here, much less knew Beckett and Arundel."

"Kray like the London crime family?" Crowley asked.

"Exactly like, yeah. Robert there is Ronnie and Reggie's nephew, I think. All part of our checkered history."

Crowley suddenly realized why the man looked familiar. Put thirty years and a few pounds on him, and he was the one looking for the dog in the hydro operation the night before. "I saw him!" Crowley said. "He's the weed grower, he was down there last night. At least, he's one of them. I imagine it's more than a one-man operation."

Morgan let out a small laugh. "True to family form, then."

"If they were mates as young men," Crowley said, "perhaps they're still mates now. So, Arundel, maybe even Beckett, might know about the weed. You think they're involved?"

"Possibly," she allowed. "But that's entirely conjecture. Even if they are still friends, it doesn't mean they know about Kray's business. Or they may know about it and choose to ignore it."

Crowley nodded. "True, there's not really any connection to be made. And this situation goes beyond the dope business anyway, right?"

Morgan nodded. "I think so. Let's not get distracted. Look at this."

She moved over to a large bookcase, filled with shelf upon shelf of leather-bound books. Gold print stamped on the spines showed there was one for each year, going back two centuries. Crowley whistled softly through his teeth.

"You'd think these should be in a museum or a humidifier or something." He reached up and took down the oldest volume, carefully opened it. It contained only handwritten notes, in a neat, looping script. Several of the oldest were the same, but Morgan checked some of the more recent ones and found they included clippings and photographs from when the Ludus Historia club had started several decades prior. It seemed the club had been included in these historical school records as equally, if not more, important.

Crowley frowned, thinking for a moment, then went back to the wall with all the group photographs. He checked the years for the photos with blacked out names and faces, then went to the bookshelf and grabbed the corresponding volumes. Morgan realized his plan and between them they started checking the books, reading the lists of member names. It took a while, but by a process of elimination they managed to identify some of the boys whose faces had been obscured. Among them Oliver Greene in 1982, Carl Masters in 1984, a few others back and forth through the years. Then Crowley pointed.

"Look here." His forefinger marked the entry for one Eric Egerton, in 1985. "This is her missing son."

Morgan nodded, licked her lips. Crowley shared her concerns. It felt like they were on the cusp of something, but he couldn't pin down quite what it was.

"Several mentions of Arundel, Beckett and Kray," Morgan said. "Accounts of activities and rituals, always signed off by the three of them, or listed as being run by all three. They seem to be the heart of the club, at least recently."

"And by recently, that means all the way back into the late 1970s," Crowley said. "Look, here in 1981."

He turned the book to show a photo of three lithe young men, shirtless and wearing bull heads. Written beneath each of them was their name – Arundel, Beckett, Kray – and under that was the word "aequinoctium."

"That's Latin," Morgan said. "It means equinox."

Above the bookcase was a large painting of Mithra slaying the bull. Crowley looked around the room, noting all the gladiator weapons hanging from the walls between paintings and photographs. More in the glass-fronted cabinets. Despite the initially Roman general feel of the place, the more attention he paid, the more apparent it became that Mithraism, rather than simply Roman history, was a focus of the club.

He opened his mouth to say more, when the door opened quickly. A curt voice said, "What are you doing in here?"

21

Tommy stared at the ancient sword, hands trembling slightly. A Roman spatha. But this was no replica like they used in the club. This was the real thing.

"The Colosseum, really?" Tommy asked.

His father nodded, smiling. "Warrior blood was spilled from that blade, onto the sands of the Colosseum, Tommy. *Millennia* ago!"

Tommy tore his gaze from the blade and looked around the vault. It was filled with artifacts. Shields and swords, spears and tridents, amphorae and chalices, coins and jewels. "These are all genuine?"

"Yes, not a replica among them. This is all history, all priceless." His father smiled sardonically. "Although occasionally we do have to put a price on something and there's always a buyer in the less reputable circles of wealth. None of this could be taken to Sotheby's, of course, but we still manage to sell a piece here and there. It's how the school remains open. And it's also how we Arundels retain our significant influence around here."

"So, it's all stolen?" Tommy asked. "It's all illegal?"

Philip Arundel sighed, shook his head. "We're preserving history."

"Even when you sell it for more power and influence? That's in the best interests of history, is it?"

"Thomas, we always vet our buyers very carefully."

Tommy knew he was pushing his luck. His father only called him Thomas when the man's patience was running thin. "I don't like it, Dad. I don't want to be a part of it anymore."

"It's your heritage, Thomas. It's your legacy!"

Tommy threw the sword down, wincing internally at

the disrespect he was showing to the ancient weapon even though he hated it. The respect for the historical value was ingrained. "It's not my legacy! Maybe it's yours, but it's not mine. I want no part of it."

"Tommy, please." His father's tone had changed again. Perhaps this was a last ditch attempt to bring him around. "This world, Tommy, is a cruel and capricious place. It eats people alive. And like any animal, the *human* animal must fight to survive. It feeds on other life, and sometimes that means other people. Sometimes we use them to put ourselves higher and survive. The elite, Tommy, will inherit the earth. That's your legacy. That's your right!"

"No, it isn't. That's just my bad luck to be born into this family. I want to live a normal life."

"Normal?" Philip snapped. "Normal like that tart from the village you knock around with? You want to be like her and dress up like a fool for the vernal equinox, Thomas? Oh yes, I know about your dalliances."

All semblance of friendliness had gone from his father's face, replaced with derision and contempt. This, Tommy realized, was his father's true face. But mention of Katie made his blood run ice cold. "You leave her out of this!"

"Or what? You really want to prance around with her in the ridiculous rituals of this backwards village? When you could be standing tall in the glory of our ancient power?"

"Dad, it's just a festival, a pageant."

His father shook his head. "Not always. Not with us. For us it's something so much more, and you want to throw it all away to be more like her?"

Tommy swallowed, but nodded. "Yes. That's actually exactly what I want. I demand my trial."

Philip Arundel's face stilled, like a lake instantly freezing over. Tommy felt a gulf open between them, an irreversible chasm. His father nodded once. "Very well."

22

Crowley's nerves spiked, then quickly settled again when he saw it was Charles Bale, one of the history club members, who had found him and Morgan snooping around. Students had no authority over teachers, even if the room had been locked. Charles, Chas to his mates, was also one of the boys who was with Tommy when Black Shuck showed up, scaring the group of truants and starting this whole thing off. And Chas went out with one of the other Academy girls, Emma, who had also been out of bounds that night. Crowley quickly logged all these details to use in case he needed to put the boy off-balance.

Crowley also noticed Chas had bruises up his forearms, and a decent swelling under his left eye. The teen looked nervous to have snapped at what turned out to be two teachers. "Sorry, Sir," he said, though it seemed an insincere apology. "Didn't realize it was you. But, er, what are you doing in here?"

"We were just looking around," Crowley said. "The club is such a large part of the school identity, I wanted to see what was in here."

"Who unlocked it for you?"

Crowley feigned surprise. "Locked? It was open when we found it." He noticed Morgan's eyes narrow slightly at his lie, but she said nothing.

"It's always kept locked," Chas said, confused.

"I guess someone forgot this time then," Crowley said. "Why is it kept locked anyway? What's so secret?"

"Oh, not secret. Just, you know, all the stuff in here is pretty valuable. It all needs to stay safe."

Crowley frowned. "Surely no one in the school would steal form its own club?"

Chas's cheeks colored a little. "Maybe not. But not everyone is in the club, and not everyone likes the club. Sir."

"It is an impressive clubhouse," Crowley said, turning to survey the space like he hadn't already been studying it in detail. "Lots of photos of stuff you've been up to, eh? What are all the trips about? Where do you go?"

"Field trips to museums quite often, Sir. And archaeological digs and metal detecting. It's one of the things I like most about the club, I get to spend a lot of time outdoors. You have to be physically fit too, so I like that as well."

"You've got some bruises there. Is that from fitness training?"

Chas licked his lips, paused a moment too long. "Yes, Sir."

He'd clearly decided that saying next to nothing was the best option after his brief moment of disclosure. "You're all obviously proud of your Roman heritage."

"It's an important part of things, yeah. It's when Britain really started to become great."

Crowley thought that was a strange and nationalistic attitude to take, but no doubt it was what the boy had been taught. As a history teacher, Crowley had started to think Britain was never Great, just great at empire-building. But they had that in common with the Romans, so perhaps it was a trait that had been passed on. "So how do I join?" he asked suddenly. "As the school's history teacher, I think maybe I should be in the history club!"

"Ah, well, it's not really that simple. Not really my place." Chas fell into an awkward silence.

Crowley frowned. This club was weird and quite plainly not really what it claimed to be. No actual history club would be so evasive. But what was it exactly? That was the question he couldn't seem to find an answer for.

"Why there are no girls in the photos?" Morgan asked.

Chas scratched his chin, looking around at the photos. "Well, it's timing to a large degree," he stammered. "The club is very old, like the school, and girls were only recently admitted to the school. You know the story, Miss. They needed the extra tuition to keep the doors open, went co-ed."

"Yes, but girls are here now and have been for a few years. So how come none have joined the club? Are they allowed?"

"I think perhaps it wouldn't really be appropriate, Miss. What with all the overnight outings, like the one tonight." Chas clammed up again.

Fishing for information, Crowley remembered the name of a young man from two years ago whose name and face had been blacked out in one of the photos. "William Tucker," he said. Chas flinched. "You remember him then?"

"Of course, Sir."

"What happened to him? Why black him out of the photos?"

Chas licked his lips, his eye twitched with a nervous tick. "He moved away, that's all. There's nothing personal in blacking out the photo. Just a silly tradition. The club has a lot of old-fashioned things like that, some of them… well, most of them, really, I don't know the reasons for. I don't know if anyone does. We black out anyone who leaves."

"Has anyone heard from Tucker?" Morgan asked. "Since he moved?"

"Not me. Why would I have?"

Morgan shrugged. "It just seems like such a close-knit club, surely someone kept in touch."

Chas scuffed his shoe against the rug, looking away. "I think so, probably. Maybe. Some boys did. I'm not sure. I wasn't close to William." He looked up, an uncomfortable expression on his face. "Tucker was an orphan, anyway. Ward of the state. He didn't have any community ties here, or any really close friends. Came to the school on a scholarship."

"What scholarship?" Morgan asked.

Chas shrugged. "The Arundel, I think."

"What about Eric Egerton?" Crowley asked. "He died

on a field trip, I heard."

Chas's face tightened up, then he nodded rapidly. "Yeah, I wasn't there."

"When it happened, you mean?"

"On that trip, I mean. I didn't go." Chas's cheeks were rosy again. Guilt of some kind, Crowley presumed.

"What happened to him, though?"

"Listen, we should lock up and go." Chas turned to the door. "I'm very sorry but I'm really not supposed to let anyone in here. And I'm in a hurry because there's an overnighter for officers of the club. I have to get ready."

They slowly headed for the door, Crowley patting the boy's shoulder. "Thanks for letting us see the artifacts and stuff," he said, keeping his tone friendly. He gave the boy's shoulder a squeeze. "I promise not to tell anyone."

Chas relaxed a little and nodded.

"Is Tommy Arundel an officer of the club?" Morgan asked casually.

"Yes," Chas said, his face immediately going red again. It seemed to embarrass or discomfort him every time they pressed for specifics. Crowley wondered what vows of secrecy they'd sworn. He thought perhaps Chas was having trouble deciding what he was allowed to divulge, but being teachers, they had him on edge.

Taking advantage of that, Crowley asked. "Is the club mascot a bull?"

Chas blinked, looking up at Crowley and then away. "Why do you ask that?"

"I saw a photo of three men wearing bull's heads."

Chas laughed, but it was a forced sound. "That's just a gag."

"They were incredibly cool-looking heads," Crowley pressed. "The craftsmanship looked remarkable. I'm a huge Halloween fan, and seeing that photo made me think it would be a fantastic Halloween costume. I'd love to get one of those bull's heads, but I suppose they weren't bought locally."

Chas fumbled in his pocket for a key and locked the

door behind him, forcing that laugh again. "I don't think they sell them anywhere, Sir. Mr. Arundel's grandfather brought them back from his travels, is what we were told."

"Travels where?"

"I've no idea, Sir."

Crowley nodded. "Well, thanks again."

"Have fun at tonight's outing," Morgan said. "What is it this time?"

"Astronomy, Miss. To celebrate the autumnal equinox."

"Ah," Crowley said, pushing for one last bite of club gossip. "Anything to do with Tauro Solis?"

Chas's ears turned scarlet, but he said, "I've never heard of that, Sir." He turned on his heel and rushed away.

23

The Leaping Hound

"I think we need to talk to the headmaster," Crowley said.

Morgan gave him an appraising look. "And say what?"

"I don't know exactly, but this club has issues and I wonder how much he knows. I want to sound him out."

Morgan pursed her lips for a moment, then nodded. "Fair enough."

The plan proved immediately fruitless when Beckett wasn't in his office or his rooms. At least, he didn't answer their knocks.

"It is Sunday, I suppose," Morgan said.

Crowley ground his teeth in frustration. "Something is up here. I need to know what. I feel like maybe tonight is important and if we just ignore this and let it go, perhaps we'll miss the chance to... I don't know. To expose something. It feels important."

"I agree, but what can we do? Clearly everyone involved is trained to keep quiet about it. Perhaps we should just let them get on with the silly club?"

Crowley shook his head. "I can't let it go that easily. Let's ask around the village. I need to connect these pieces. Were you happy with Chas's answers about the Tucker kid? Or Egerton?"

"Not really," Morgan said. "He seemed evasive. Maybe he really doesn't know and it bothers him. But what can we do about that?"

"Let's ask the cops. Particularly about the Egerton death. That one is really bothering me."

Morgan was surprised, but she seemed almost amused too. Crowley didn't mind, he was glad to have her along even if she was only humoring him. He could be a bit of a terrier with things like this. If he felt something was going on or there was more to learn, he clamped his jaws on and wouldn't let go. Shake something enough and things usually started to fall out.

There was only one policeman on duty in the small village station when they arrived, a middle-aged man with a balding head and narrow eyes. Crowley took an instant dislike to the fellow, but smiled, trying to temper his reaction.

"Help you?" the policeman said. His name badge read Senior Constable Barry Jenkins.

"This will seem a little out of left field," Crowley said. "But I wanted to ask you something about an old case. We're teachers from up at the academy, and were wondering about the death of Eric Egerton, one of the students there."

"What about it?"

"Well, I wondered if it was resolved. Is it still an open case? Was there an official verdict on the death? Accidental?"

"No idea."

"Can you look it up? How he died?"

"I can't talk about anything like that with you." Jenkins smiled, but it was cold. Unkind. "Police business."

"Right."

The two men stared at each other for a moment.

Morgan stepped forward. "We're concerned about the activities of the history club up at the school. Can you tell us how Eric died? We're mainly trying to make sure nothing like that ever happens again, that's all." She smiled warmly, even leaned forward a little, playing up the sweet damsel angle, Crowley thought.

But Jenkins was a rock not for cracking. "Don't know anything about the case, couldn't tell you if I did. I suggest you let it go. I'm sure the club has its own concerns in order."

"What makes you say that?" Crowley asked. "Maybe they don't. How would you know?"

"I would suggest, sir, that if you don't know anything about the club, perhaps that's how they want it. You want to know more, join up. In the meantime, mind your business."

Crowley frowned at him, wondering why the man was so hostile about it. Was he involved? How deep through the village did all this go? "Are you in the club?" he asked. "Did you go to the Academy?"

Jenkins stood up straight, sniffed. "I'm a busy man and you're wasting police time." He turned and walked away into the back office, leaving the front desk unattended.

Crowley and Morgan exchanged a bemused look. She grinned, then couldn't suppress a short laugh. Crowley smirked back. "Friendly bloke," he said.

"Excellent public relations," she agreed.

They left the station and Crowley said, "I bet he's friends with Arundel. This whole village is too close knit for my liking."

"I know what you mean."

"Drink?"

Morgan looked at him, one eyebrow raised.

"It's Sunday afternoon," Crowley said. "Excellent time for a pint. Plus, people in the pub tend to be chatty. Might pick up some gossip there. It's not a date, if that's what you're worried about."

Morgan rolled her eyes, but smiled again. "Come on then."

It was a short walk to the pub, and the place was busy with locals.

"Hey up, here's trouble."

Crowley nodded to Ian Barnes, the old storyteller he'd chatted to before. "How are you?"

"I'm well. Teachers coming here so often, has the academy lowered its standards?"

"Maybe we've raised them," Crowley said. "This is Elizabeth Morgan, a colleague from school."

"Pleased to meet you, Miss."

"You too." She gave Crowley a sidelong glance.

He leaned close and quickly whispered. "He's one of the chatty ones." More loudly he said, "Can we join you?"

Barnes seemed surprised but gestured to his otherwise empty table. "Please do."

"What are you drinking?" Crowley asked.

"Pint of bitter, thanks."

Crowley turned to Morgan. "And you, Elizabeth?"

She sat, looking slightly annoyed but playing along. "House red is fine."

"Be right back."

Crowley went to the bar and ordered the drinks, a second pint of bitter for himself. The place was quite busy, the leftovers from the Sunday lunch crowd hanging around to enjoy a few more drinks, the atmosphere warm and collegiate. Everyone he passed gave him a glance, but no real animosity or suspicion was on display. Perhaps they were growing used to him. Rupert and his father were nowhere to be seen, however. Crowley didn't think he'd be so warmly welcomed by them.

When he returned to the table, Barnes was saying, "Oh, there's all kinds of scandals you lot cover up all the time!" At Morgan's surprised look, he added, "Well, not you personally. But the academy bigwigs. You know what I mean."

"Arundel, you mean?" Crowley asked, placing the drinks around and sitting down. "Or Beckett?"

"Well, both. But like I told you before, Beckett only does what Arundel tells him."

"What got you onto this subject?" Crowley asked.

Barnes laughed. "Miss Morgan here—"

"Elizabeth, please."

"As you wish. Elizabeth here was asking why so many people down here in the village seem to scoff at the school and the teachers. So I was talking about some of the things that have happened over the years. Your school has a checkered past."

Crowley took the opportunity. "Funny you should say that. We were talking earlier about Eric Egerton. Young lad who died on a school outing."

"That's as good an example as any."

"What do you mean?"

Barnes gave a half smile. "Died on a school outing, you say. That's the official line, but it's not true, is it."

"No?"

"Egerton was on scholarship to the school. Rumor was his mother was sleeping with Arundel, which is how the boy was admitted and his tuition was covered. He died, and they say it was an accident on a history club outing, but I question if it was an accident at all. You ask Millie and she'll tell you it was no accident."

"I have chatted to her," Crowley said. "She seems like a very sad and lonely woman."

"Stopped seeing Arundel right when Eric died. Pretty much been a hermit ever since. She wants justice, but knows she'll never get it."

"Justice?" Morgan asked. "For what?"

"For the fact it was probably no accident that Eric died. He was mercilessly bullied by the rich kids in the club, so the word around here says. They gave him a hard time, treated him terribly. I used to do some extra work up at the academy grounds and I saw Eric the day before he died. The day before that outing. All I know for certain is Eric was very upset that day, and didn't want to go on the outing. He went to his mother and begged to quit the school and move away. I asked him why they didn't and he said his mother had told him they couldn't pull up stakes and leave. She told him he wasn't going to ruin his chance to better himself, and to toughen up."

"So they stayed and Eric died," Morgan said, almost a whisper. "Poor Millie!"

"Yep. She never forgave herself."

"I was asking Millie about the club and some of the things that go on around here," Crowley said. "She said to me that I should look to the pub. What do you think she meant by that?"

Barnes shrugged and looked away, then made a big deal of having a long drink from his pint. "Don't know what she means there," he said eventually. "Except not much goes on around here without word of it passing through the Hound. And of course, all those snobs like Arundel and Beckett come here all the time for a drink only to remind us of our place with their swanky ways."

"Do you know anything about Tauro Solis?" Crowley asked.

Barnes frowned, shook his head. Crowley wasn't sure if the man was being straight with him about that. Before he could press the point, he noticed Barnes was looking up and past him. The old man's eyes had widened in concern.

Crowley turned to see that several people had moved in behind them. Three of them were the thugs he had fought, Rupert in particular looking furious, plus a few other toughs.

"Help you, fellas?" he asked, mind churning with possibilities. They had him at a distinct disadvantage, sitting as he was.

"Someone wants to talk to you," Rupert said. "How about you and your friend come with us?"

"Jake?" Morgan said nervously.

Barnes was staring at his pint, gripped tight in a trembling hand.

"I don't think so," Crowley said with a tight smile. "But I'm happy to chat here. Why don't you tell whoever it is to come and join us. I'll buy them a drink."

"Oh, you misunderstand. This isn't a request. Get up."

24

The Leaping Hound

Crowley stood, tense, his hands involuntarily clenched into fists. He'd had no trouble with three of these young goons before, but there were several more now and they were cornered in the pub. A number of the locals watched on, curious but otherwise seemingly unbothered. Morgan stood beside him.

"This way," Rupert said.

Crowley saw something in the boy's eye then, a kind of pleading. He was acting tough, but seemed desperate.

"Jake?" Morgan said again.

"It's okay," he said quietly. "It'll be fine." He turned to Barnes. "Thanks for the chat. We'll catch up again soon."

Barnes raised his pint in acknowledgement, but not his eyes, staring resolutely at the scuffed tabletop.

Rupert and his friends led Crowley and Morgan down past the bar and along a short passage to a wooden door. Rupert opened the door, then stepped back to gesture Crowley and Morgan in. It was a large walk-in closet, filled with cleaning supplies, paper goods, bar towels and more. A young woman was waiting.

"You're Katie," Morgan said in surprise. "Tommy Arundel's girlfriend, right?"

Katie smiled nervously and nodded. She pointed to one of Rupert's cohorts. "And his sister," she said.

Rupert and a couple of others came into the cramped space and closed the door, leaving the rest to their own devises outside. "Sorry for the menacing approach," Rupert said. "But there'd be trouble if we acted friendly-like to you. In public."

Crowley frowned. "Okay. What's this all about then?"

"I think Tommy is in danger," Katie said. "And I think

it has something to do with the history club."

This strengthened Crowley's conviction that something was far awry in Market Scarston at this point in time. "I'm glad you trusted me to talk to," he said. "I'm sure you're right. But what danger?"

"I can't give many details, to be honest. But Tommy has been acting strangely. He's upset with his dad and concerned about the school and the club. He told me he just wants to run away and leave it all behind, and asked if I'd go with him. I told him it wasn't that easy and he got a bit angry. He told me he'd be earning his freedom tonight and I should think seriously about whether I wanted to stay here. I asked him what on earth he was talking about but he clammed up then and got defensive. I could tell one thing for certain and that's that he was scared. It's not like Tommy to be scared of anything."

Crowley paused, running over in his mind all that he'd learned. He looked up and said, "I talked to Millie Egerton recently."

Katie made a noise of distress. "Eric died!"

"I know. I asked her about it and she was evasive, but she kept saying that I should look to the pub. What does that mean, do you think?"

Katie shook her head. "Not sure."

"Tunnels, maybe?" Rupert suggested.

Kate brightened up. "Oh yeah, maybe! I bet it has something to do with the tunnels."

"And the weed business?" Crowley asked.

Katie's eyes widened. "I'm surprised you know about that. How did you–"

Crowley held up a hand, also ignoring Rupert's suddenly scarlet cheeks. "Don't worry about how I know. I'm not really bothered about the weed itself. But could that be part of the problem? People can get violent and make bad decisions around illegal enterprises like that."

Katie frowned, shook her head. "I don't think it's really related to the club though. I mean, except that Kray works for Arundel and runs the weed business for him, and Kray is also a high officer in the club. Has been since their school days, I think. But the weed business is a sideline, probably most of the people in the club know nothing about it. But the tunnels go other places too. They lead to some place the history club only goes on very special occasions. Tommy told me it's a place called the Sanctum. He used to think it was pretty cool, but maybe he's changed his mind about that now?"

"Where is it?"

"I'm not sure exactly where it is, but I know the club often meets here at the pub, or behind the pub in the car park. Everyone knows that somewhere around there is one of the ways into the tunnels, but no one would dare tell, or go down there without permission."

"So maybe that's what Millie Egerton meant when she told me to look here," Crowley mused. "And perhaps it's also the way to the Sanctum?"

"Maybe. I know they regularly meet at Arundel's big house too, and I expect there's more ways in and out from there too. I think Tommy said they were starting at the estate tonight, but that doesn't mean it's the only way to the Sanctum, if it's down there. It's a warren of old passages under this village."

"You don't know anything more about it?"

"No. Oh, except Tommy always talks about the sign of the bull." She made the sign of the horns with her fingers, then shrugged again.

Crowley remembered the engraving he'd seen halfway to the weed operation before. And the mosaic that had gone missing. The mystery of what exactly Tauro Solis was. The Mithras trapping, always around the bull motif. It was all connected, but he couldn't place why or how. Although it seemed that this night was a special occasion, being the vernal equinox, and perhaps this Sanctum place was where the club would be acting out its rituals. And if Tommy was indeed in danger, then Crowley didn't have much time to find out where he needed to go.

"Why are you helping us?" he asked.

"We hate the school," Katie said. "Us village kids, I mean. It's elitism of the worst kind, and we don't really like you for being part of it."

Crowley couldn't help but accept that. He was rapidly reconsidering his career choices. Perhaps a nice public school in the city somewhere would be a better place to ply his new trade. Somewhere he could make a difference where kids weren't born into this kind of privilege. But that was a concern for another day. "But?" he prompted.

"But I love Tommy." Katie gestured to the others crammed in the small space. "We all like Tommy, he's not like the others. Not all the students are like their parents."

"They usually end up like them though," Rupert said bitterly. "The school turns them."

"Seems like there's a lot of cliques around this village," Morgan said. "We asked about Eric Egerton at the police station and got rudely brushed off."

"Jenkins?" one young man asked.

"Yeah," Crowley said. "You know him? Who are you?"

"My name's Marcus. Tommy's a good mate. But you'll get no help from Jenkins. He's in Arundel's pocket, just like most of the locals. Besides, you'd never prove anything about Eric, that's all gone long cold." Marcus's face hardened. "But there's still time to help Tommy."

Crowley nodded. It was time, he decided, to get pro-active about all this. He knew a way down into the tunnels, at least. "I know where to begin," he said. "I don't suppose any of you have a weapon I can borrow?"

A few eyes widened among a general shaking of heads.

"A weapon?" Morgan asked.

"I like to be prepared. Give me a minute." He found an old canvas backpack on a shelf, the kind scouts might have used back in the 60s. It seemed sturdy enough. He grabbed several items off the shelves, bundled them up inside the old bag, then slung it onto his shoulders.

"What are going to do with all that?" Morgan asked.

He shrugged. "Hopefully nothing, but like I said, I like to be prepared. I learned in the serviced that planning is the most important part of any mission."

"The service, eh?" Morgan said with a smile.

He smiled back, but didn't reply. Privately, he wished he had some weapons just to be safe. But he'd have to make do. "Right. I'm off."

"I'm coming too," Morgan said. Her expression brooked no argument.

"Okay, then." He turned back to Katie and the others. "Thanks for your help. You did the right thing coming to me. I promise I'll do all I can to take care of Tommy. And perhaps it's time the history club was itself history."

He left the closet and Morgan followed him out of the pub. "Where are we supposed to start?"

"Follow me." Crowley led her through the car park and around to the back of the pub. Casting a quick glance around to make sure no one was watching, he crouched and set to work to unlock the doors down into the old basement.

"Well, I wasn't expecting that," Morgan said as he gestured for her to descend.

Once they were inside, he closed the trapdoor and clicked on his flashlight. "This way."

He led her to the next trapdoor and before long they were down in the tunnels under Market Scarston.

"You are a man of many surprises, Jake Crowley," Morgan said. "How did you know about all this?"

He grinned, but headed off without answering. Soon he was shining his light on the old engraving of the bull.

"I think this is what Tommy was talking about, when he said the sign of the bull."

Morgan looked around the dark tunnels. "But there's nothing here."

"I was thinking about that map we looked at," Crowley said. "The old taurobolium Tommy fell into is over that way some few hundred yards. The weed operation is back that way, in an old cave that's connected to these tunnels." He pointed obliquely between the two directions. "And that is Arundel's estate. If there's some way to get between the old taurobolium and the weed cave, in that direction, we'd be right under Arundel's land. If all these caves and tunnels are linked up, maybe the link is this Sanctum Katie told us about."

"And perhaps that tunnel with the mosaic also links to the Sanctum, which is why they quickly collapsed it," Morgan said. "No time to take any chances."

"Right. Or it might lead to the marijuana operation. Either way, best to quickly shut it off. And I expect the mosaic was worth too much to destroy, so they quickly took that way first. It's probably safe somewhere at Arundel's place by now. It occurs to me now that perhaps the mosaic was a door, but that it only opened from the other side. That taurobolium was a dead end otherwise."

Morgan nodded. "That all makes sense. But how do we prove it? How do we get further?"

Crowley ran his hands over the walls, knocked on the old stonework. "There must be a secret passage or some kind of door here. Help me look."

Morgan lit up her phone and between them they began exploring every part of the tunnels around the old sign. A low growl caught Crowley's ear and he froze.

"Don't panic," he said quietly. "But there's a huge dog down here, and it's dusted with something to make it glow red."

"Are you serious?"

"It's to protect the marijuana farm, that's all. I'm sure it's not always here, but it was before and I think it's back."

Morgan returned to what she'd been doing, busily scraping at the stonework. The sound of skittering paws echoed along towards them, getting closer. The growl grew louder, and deeper.

"Damn it!" Crowley snapped, and he started to shrug off the backpack, about to improvise a weapon. Given the size of the dog, he worried he didn't have anything good enough. The growling got closer still and he made out the silhouette of the giant hound bearing down on them.

"Aha!" Morgan said.

She pushed hard on something and a grinding came

from the wall beside Crowley. He chanced a glance and saw the section of wall with the engraving on it had popped open an inch. Morgan dragged on it and it opened like a door.

She ducked inside and Crowley followed, swiftly closing the door behind them just as the dog pounced. It crashed into the stone and barked in pained annoyance.

"Well done!" he said.

Morgan smiled. "Now what?"

25

Beneath Market Scarston

They stood for a moment, listening to the large dog clawing and snuffling on the other side of the door. The tunnel they were in headed straight ahead, ancient like the ones Crowley had found himself in after escaping the taurobolium before. The ground seemed level.

"This way then, I suppose," he said.

He set off with his torchlight playing over the walls ahead of him. He heard Morgan's steps close behind. "What do you think we'll find?" she asked, speaking in a low whisper.

"I don't know. But whatever this Sanctum is that Katie talked about, I'm hoping it'll be this way and answer some of our questions."

"Too many bloody questions!" a gruff voice ahead snarled. A large man moved into the passage ahead of them.

"Kray!" Morgan said.

It was the large blond man Crowley had seen before in the marijuana farm. He had a good six inches on Crowley's six-foot frame, and he seemed more heavily muscled too. He was an imposing presence, and his teeth were bared in anger. "I can't believe you got away when I dropped a grenade on you!" he said, his voice low and guttural.

"That was you?" Crowley said in surprise, though perhaps he shouldn't be so shocked. The man had a violent ancestry, after all.

"It wasn't under Arundel's orders or anything, but I took my chance. I found some old World War II surplus down in the tunnels a while back and when I saw you skulking around I thought I'd do some tidying up. How did you survive that, anyway?"

Crowley grinned, despite his nerves. Best to play up

whatever concerns this guy might have. "You'd be amazed what I've survived, old son." In truth, he did have some stories to tell.

Kray made a noise of anger, not unlike his dog, and said, "Well, you won't survive now!" He rushed forward, lifting a broad-bladed knife into view.

Crowley cursed. That was bad odds. He remembered his old hand-to-hand combat sergeant in the SAS.

What do you do when a man draws a knife on you, Crowley?
Shoot him, Sergeant!
And if you don't have a gun?
I run away, Sergeant!
And if you can't run away?

At that point, Crowley was out of answers. He knew being unarmed in a knife fight was a bad position to be in, but he didn't want to venture a guess.

The sergeant grinned at him. *You get cut, Crowley, that's what! The thing you have to decide is where and how you get cut to give you the best chance of bringing the bastard down right afterwards.*

With that in mind, Crowley whipped his backpack around and held it up like a shield just as Kray reached him and slammed down an overhead strike with the big knife. Better to get his gear stabbed than himself. As the long blade got tangled in the canvas, Crowley twisted it and dragged Kray's arm sideways, pulling the large man off balance. As Kray tried to sidestep, Crowley stamped out a powerful, low kick to the side of the man's knee. There was a sickening crunch and Kray howled in pain, falling sideways up against the passage wall.

Crowley wasted no time, stepping straight up to Kray and swinging another heavy kick, this time into the big man's stomach. The air rushed out of him, and he curled up around Crowley's foot. Despite his pain and injuries, he was tenacious. He twisted his arms and body, trying to bring Crowley down with him.

Crowley wasn't about to allow that. He shifted his weight and dropped his knee into Kray's ribs. He was rewarded with another dull crack. Kray roared in pain, face twisted and red, teeth bared. But he still didn't let go.

Then Morgan was there. She stepped up next to them and brought something whistling through the air, down onto the side of Kray's head. There was a dull thunk and the man fell instantly still.

Crowley untangled himself and retrieved his flashlight. Morgan stood there holding the ten-inch wrench he'd packed into the backpack earlier. "Not the reason I brought it along, but a damn fine usage all the same," he said, grinning.

"It fell out of the hole the knife made in the bag," Morgan said. She gave it to him with a shaking hand. "Have I killed him?"

"No, someone like him has a pretty thick skull, I'd say. He'll have a hell of a concussion though." Crowley scrabbled in the bag and pulled out a coil of nylon rope. "I'm glad I brought this too."

Kray began to writhe and moan as Crowley quickly bound his hands and feet, trussing him up like a Christmas turkey. His eyes were glazed and blood leaked from the gash in his head where Morgan had hit him, but he still managed to spit some eloquent curses at them both.

"Where's the Sanctum?" Crowley demanded.

Kray made an incredibly disparaging remark about Crowley's mother. It was obvious he wasn't about to answer any questions. Crowley dragged him back along the passage a way then returned to Morgan. "Come on, let's keep going."

They hurried along, lights playing over the stone. They soon reached a set of stairs leading down, then the passage levelled out again and continued for another several hundred feet. They heard muffled shouting up ahead.

Crowley looked at Morgan and smiled. "Perhaps we're on the right track."

They continued along and before much further the passage ahead was lit with a soft, orange glow. They doused their lights and moved more slowly, crouching low as they approached a well-lit opening at the end of the tunnel.

They emerged onto a stone terrace looking down into a huge torchlit chamber.

Morgan sucked in a shocked breath as they both ducked back into the shadows, then whispered, "Oh my God!"

26

The Sanctum

They looked down upon a massive stone chamber. It had to be more than fifty feet across, torches burning in sconces all around the walls. The center, low down, was a circular fighting pit with a packed dirt floor. In concentric circles around the pit were four levels of terraces, making the whole place into an amphitheater. On the far side, another tunnel like the one Crowley and Morgan hunkered down in led away into darkness. That one, Crowley was prepared to bet, would lead to Arundel's estate.

Symbols of Mithraism decorated the walls, stone carvings of impressive workmanship. On the wall to their left was a huge engraving of the bull and sun symbol of Tauro Solis, worked into the tightly fitted stones. To their right side was a similarly huge carving of Mithras slaying the bull.

The circular fighting pit had a ring of flagstones around its edge, and engraved twice on those stones, once each side to encircle the pit, was the legend *moritūrī tē salūtant*. Crowley recognized the quote from Roman history, he had learned it long before Hollywood co-opted it. *Those who are about to die salute you.*

The Sanctum was packed with people too. Crowley recognized several boys from the school, among many other people of varying ages. Lots of older men from the village were present. All were clad in togas, all were shouting and chanting. Then a loud metallic clanging sounded over the voices.

Crowley saw the headmaster, Archie Beckett. He held a round metal shield and was striking it with the flat of a Roman spatha. The gathering slowly fell silent.

Crowley crouched lower, Morgan beside him. "Let's see

what they get up to before we interrupt, shall we?"

She nodded, brow furrowed. "They seem to be taking everything very seriously."

"Quite the history club!"

"Welcome!" Beckett intoned, his voice loud and imperious. "Before we begin tonight's equinox ritual, there is another matter to attend to. The weapons?"

A boy ran forward and placed two spatha in the center of the fighting pit, their blades crossed in an X, then scurried away again. Cheers and whoops rose up, then settled quickly as Beckett once again spoke.

"Thomas Arundel?"

Tommy stepped forward from the crowd, his face dark. He looked smaller than usual, cowed and saddened. He said something Crowley couldn't hear.

"Loud enough for all, please!" Beckett demanded.

Tommy looked up and anger replaced the melancholy expression on his face. "I demand trial by combat!"

"Thomas Arundel has expressed his desire to leave us," Beckett said. "There is only one way out of the Sanctum. The weapons are ready. Who will be the Champion of the Sanctum for this trial?"

"I will."

Philip Arundel stepped forward, his face thunderous. He sneered across the circle of the pit at his son and Tommy blanched at the sight of his father's disdain.

"Dad? What are you doing?"

"Expected to fight one of your school friends, did you?" Arundel asked. His voice dripped with contempt. "You thought you'd play act a sparring match then walk away? You've never realized how serious this business is. But you know what? I'm glad. In the eyes if Mithras, spilling the blood of the son grants eternal life." He grinned, wolfish. His eyes sparkled.

"Are you serious?" Tommy asked, but his voice had weakened again.

"Yes, I am." Philip Arundel threw off his toga, to reveal nothing but a loin cloth beneath. His body was fit and lean, accentuated by his tall frame, muscular and hard.

Tommy shook his head, disbelief evident. He dropped his own toga, also revealing a loincloth and nothing else. He was fit too, strong and athletic like his father, but he wasn't yet a man, his body still juvenile. Crowley couldn't imagine the boy stood a chance against his father, bigger, stronger, and far more skilled.

As the crowd yelled and cheered, Crowley turned to Morgan. "He's completely mad! Tommy is going to be the human sacrifice. Philip actually believes this stuff!"

Morgan stared, mouth open in horror. "We have to do something!" she said.

Crowley nodded. "We do. And now I'm glad I prepared. But this will take me a minute." He opened the canvas backpack again and started pulling things out. Chlorine bleach in plastic bottles, home brand cleaning solutions, some screw-top glass jars.

"What are you doing?" Morgan asked.

"I'm making a distraction. Once I launch these, I'm going to go for Arundel and you need to get to Tommy and get out of there."

Morgan frowned at him, but nodded. "Whatever it is, just hurry!"

Crowley held his breath, quickly mixing chemicals and tightening the jar lids on. He heard the clang of swords and the cheers of the crowd. The fight had started.

As he worked swiftly, Crowley kept glancing up to see what was happening. It was clear that Arundel was toying with Tommy. The man's skills far exceeded those of his son, and Tommy was still banged up from his fall. He moved awkwardly, stiffly. Obviously it wasn't enough for Philip to beat his son, he had to humiliate him too. The man was pure evil. The crowd cheered, probably misinterpreting Arundel's half-hearted efforts. They yelled for Tommy to stick it to Arundel, shouted tips and encouragement. Several were also cheering on the elder man. Several older villagers had looks of covetous greed on their face and Crowley realized it was actual bloodlust.

Crowley finished mixing up the chemicals and had three large jars ready to launch. "Here goes nothing!" he said, and hurled a jar down among the assembled crowd where they were gathered together the thickest on the far side of the pit. It smashed on the stone floor. He threw another into the far side of the crowd, leaving only the exit out the opposite tunnel clear. The third he managed to smash right at Philip Arundel's feet.

Shouts and confusion erupted, people began shrieking and coughing.

"Homemade chlorine gas," Crowley told Morgan with a grin. "Try not to breathe it in. Come on!"

She shook her head, half a grin pulling at her lips. Crowley was pleased with how he had managed to impress her a few times with his entirely un-teacher-like skills. He was starting to like her more and more.

Morgan lifted her shirt over her nose and mouth and together they ran down into the fighting pit. The onlookers fled, all in a hurry to leave the sanctum, pushing and shoving each other as they bolted down the opposite tunnel and away. But Philip Arundel, despite coughs and streaming eyes, was still fighting Tommy. His son staggered under a vicious onslaught of sword strikes, barely able to fend them off. The boy would not last much longer. Arundel seemed to hardly notice the gas, lips pulled back in a determined grimace.

As Crowley gained the dirt floor of the pit, he saw Arundel knock the sword from Tommy's hand. The older man grinned and drew his weapon back to deliver a killing blow.

Tommy stood his ground, chest out, arms hanging at his side. His face was wet with sweat, but his eyes defiant. "Do it!" he yelled at his father. "Finish the job!" His eyes streamed and he coughed.

Arundel paused, looking at his son with some sadness. "I wish it didn't have to be this way."

"Do you?" Tommy said. "Didn't you say I was always a disappointment to you?"

Arundel grinned again. "That's true." He reversed his grip on the sword, holding it with both hands, raised to stab down into Tommy's neck the way a gladiator would finish a kill.

It was the only moment Crowley needed, hammering across the pit in a full-out sprint.

"Stop!" Beckett yelled between coughs, the only crowd member left. But Arundel wasn't listening.

Crowley leaped, flying through the air as Arundel began to drive the sword down. He collided with the tall man, his shoulder slamming into Arundel's side, and they both tumbled to the ground. Crowley rolled away as Arundel sprang gracefully to his feet, still holding his sword.

"You!" Anger at first, then he smiled at the sight of Crowley, crouched and weaponless. "Well, perhaps this is fortuitous, after all." His eyes were red and streaming, he coughed and his breath rasped in his throat. But he levelled his sword and advanced. "I have rather been looking forward to meeting you again."

27

The Sanctum

"Jake!"

Crowley glanced up past Arundel's shoulder and saw Morgan. She was dragging Tommy by one hand, but in her other she held the sword the student had dropped. She threw it, up in a high arc.

Arundel thought to take advantage of Crowley's distraction, lunging forward. Crowley ducked, spun on one knee to avoid Arundel's sweeping blade, then stood and snatched Tommy's sword from the air. Arundel was fast, already switching back his attack. Crowley managed to sweep his blade around just in time to deflect the blow, the swords ringing high and clear. The vibration rattled through Crowley's wrist right up to his elbow, but he'd bought himself a moment. He backed up and the two men slowly circled each other, legs bent ready to pounce, eyes locked.

"Go!" Crowley called out. "Get Tommy out of here."

The gas was dissipating, but not quickly enough. His eyes burned, his nose itched, his throat felt raw. He suppressed coughs while he watched Arundel. The man's face was red, his eyes like Black Shuck's from the legends, tears soaked his cheeks. His breath whistled in a tight throat and he repeatedly coughed, short and shallow. But he seemed unbothered by it all, his focus unbroken.

"There's nowhere you can go that I won't find you, son," Arundel said in a strident voice, without taking his eyes from Crowley's. The effect was partially lost in the wheeze of the man's tone, but the malice was evident. "I'll be directly along right behind you as soon as I dispatch this schoolteacher." He spat the word like it was a curse, and had no fear of his opponent.

That was okay with Crowley. Arundel clearly

underestimated who he was up against. Crowley had a history that might make this man blanche. Then again, despite training in all sorts of combat, including some Japanese Kendo swordsmanship, he could hardly be called a swordsman. But he was athletic, quick on his feet, strong, with good reflexes. And not much in the way of fear. He didn't look to see if Morgan had indeed left with Tommy, he simply assumed she had, as Arundel lunged again.

He circled his blade around again, interrupting Arundel's attack, then leaped desperately straight up as Arundel reversed his assault and went for Crowley's legs. Crowley barely managed to keep his feet on his ankles, but had millimeters to spare then landed hard. He twisted away, ducking and back-pedaling to buy space. Arundel was relentless in his forward motion. Crowley knew the edge of the pit was close and he didn't want to end up pinned against it, so he smashed Arundel's sword aside with all the strength he could muster, then whipped his blade around in a swift figure eight. His opponent was more surprised than threatened and simply leaned briefly back from the whirling attempt, but it bought Crowley a moment to duck and roll past Arundel. He gained the middle of the pit again and the two men once more warily circled each other.

"You simply delay the inevitable, Crowley," Arundel said with a sneer, then a cough. "I will enjoy gutting you like a trout."

The gas seemed to have mostly cleared and Crowley blinked, his vision slowly coming clear again. The wide-open sanctum was empty except for himself and Arundel, and one other person up on the terrace to his left.

"Philip, please!" the man said, and Crowley realized it was Archie Beckett, the headmaster still here, his voice wheedling. "This has gone too far!"

Arundel barked a laugh, then swept two quick alternating chops to either side. Crowley danced back from the first, blocked the second, and nearly dropped his sword. He backed up again. "This is barely beginning!" Arundel said.

"Philip, this is not what Ludus Historia is about!"

Arundel paused to cast a bemused glance up at the man. "This is exactly what it's about, you fool!"

Crowley seized the moment and rushed forward, but Arundel was not so foolish as to be genuinely distracted. Without even looking back at Crowley he swept his sword around, point down, knocking Crowley's blade aside as he thrust it for the man's ribs. Before he could turn the blade over into a counterstrike, Crowley jumped back. Arundel's skills with swordplay were incredible and he greatly outmatched his opponent. Crowley needed more time, more distractions, and a plan.

"We fight, of course," Beckett said. "But we don't kill!"

"Oh, so shut up, Bucket!" Arundel turned his full attention back to Crowley, advancing again. He had a murderous finality in his eyes and Crowley realized he was done playing and was coming in for the kill.

"You've killed plenty of people!" Crowley said, directing his anger at Arundel but hoping his words would reach Beckett. He needed the man's help, not his whining protestations. "Oliver Greene, for example," Crowley said. "William Tucker too? And Eric Egerton!" He moved fast, circling, forcing Arundel to chase him around the pit.

"Now, that's not true," Beckett said. "Greene left the club. And Egerton's death was an accident."

"Think of all the boys who have left the club," Crowley shouted, circling again, ready to duck and roll once more. "Have you ever seen them since? Even one of them?"

Arundel grinned, lunged, but Crowley saw it coming and twisted aside. He didn't try to attack any more, or even defend himself and stay close. He just kept moving.

"They were required to move away," Beckett said. "That's in the charter of the club." But his voice had weakened. It was obvious he has his doubts.

"Convenient, no?" Crowley said. "You ever check on any of them?" He grinned. It was clear he was making Arundel angry and that could cause the man to make a mistake.

"Philip, tell this man he's wrong!" Beckett pleaded.

Arundel snarled and attacked Crowley, rushing in. Crowley managed to clumsily parry just in time, and the two of them ended up closer than before. On autopilot, Crowley whipped up his left arm, cracking his elbow across the bridge of Arundel's nose. It made a satisfying crack and blood flooded over Arundel's top lip.

Arundel grunted in pain and took one step back, but seemed barely fazed by the blow. He immediately drove forward on the attack again. Crowley desperately side-stepped then ran crabwise around the edge of the pit. "You murdered them, didn't you, Arundel! Those teenage boys. And how many more?"

"This can't be true!" Beckett insisted. "The club exists to preserve history, that's all."

"And to preserve its secrets," Crowley said.

He and Arundel clashed again. This time Crowley pressed into the attack, trying to get close enough to nullify the use of Arundel's blade. The elbow he'd landed before had given him confidence. He tried to knee Arundel in the groin but the tall man turned his leg, deflected the blow, and tried to crack Crowley between the eyes with the pommel on the hilt of his sword.

Crowley turned his head, and the hard metal scraped along the side near his temple, the pain sharp. He had a flash of dizziness from the blow and shoved hard against Arundel's chest to make space between them again.

"Philip, please, stop this!"

Arundel staggered, a laugh briefly devolving into a cough that he quickly suppressed. "Oh, do grow up, Bucket! The club's secrets can never be allowed to get out. What if people in Wellisle found out, eh?" He coughed again, frowning as he tried to clear his throat. The dose of gas he'd got had obviously had a bigger effect than he'd at first allowed and he was beginning to suffer more from its ongoing effect. But he pressed on, determined to ignore it. "If a few defectors have to die to protect those secrets, so be it!"

"Why didn't you tell me? We're partners!"

"Come on, Bucket! You never could see how things really are! You're a fool. A useful fool, but you don't have what it really takes. You never did."

He circled away from Crowley, trying to clear his throat. His breathing was tight and Crowley realized it was the effort of the fight that made the effects of the gas more pronounced. The more puffed out Arundel became, the more the gas prevented him from regaining his breath. Smiling, Crowley pressed the attack again, sweeping his blade in big, powerful arcs to make Arundel move quickly, expend more energy.

"You really did kill Oliver Greene?" Becket asked, his voice high with disbelief.

"Of course he did!" Crowley said.

"But he gave his word..."

Arundel laughed, then stopped as coughing wracked him again. "As if a person's word means anything. It's actions that count, always." He growled, angry with Crowley, and counterattacked, driving forward. Crowley hurried back, made Arundel chase him again. As the tall man tried to suck breath in, he coughed again and slowed. He paused, still overconfident. "Besides, I never fully trusted you, Beckett," he said.

"You're just a useful lackey, Headmaster," Crowley added.

"It's not true!" Beckett shouted. There was the singing ring of metal as Beckett drew his own sword.

Crowley grinned. *That's it*, he thought. *Come and bloody help me! Prove you're not useless.*

Arundel heard the weapon being drawn and tried harder to end the fight. Despite his tightness of breath he launched a furious attack, blow after blow. Crowley blocked the first, then the second, but the third knocked his sword arm wide. The fourth came down and Crowley barely had time to bring his weapon back and Arundel's strike knocked the spatha from Crowley's hand, his fingers instantly numb. With nothing left to lose, Crowley drove down and forward.

Arundel's blade came straight in and Crowley felt a line of fire sear along his left ribs. Ignoring it, he drove his shoulder into Arundel and forced the man backwards.

He felt Arundel's arms rise up, imagined the man's sword reversed, point down aiming right between his shoulder blade. With a roar of effort, Crowley drove his legs into the ground and slammed Arundel back into the stone terrace.

Beckett stood there above them both, his faced twisted in hurt and anger. His sword came around and knocked Arundel's blade aside, saving Crowley's life at the last possible second. Crowley tipped himself sideways and Beckett turned his own blade over, point down.

"This ends!" he yelled and drove his weapon hard into Arundel's chest. It punched right through and scraped into the stone beneath. Arundel's breath whooshed out and he curled up around the sword, eyes wide in pain and surprise.

He fell back as Crowley scrambled away. Arundel's fingers clawed at the metal sticking out of his chest. He tipped his head back, staring up at Beckett in astonishment. He tried to say something, his lips moving, but only blood bubbled up and speckled his face.

Beckett leaned down, close enough to kiss the man, and said, "My name is not Bucket."

28

The Sanctum

"Mr. Crowley, are you okay?" Beckett jumped down, not looking at Arundel who lay bent backwards over the stone terrace staring sightlessly up at the domed ceiling.

Crowley pulled himself into a sitting position, pulling in long breaths to settle his burning lungs. He gingerly lifted the side of his shirt, which had become drenched with blood, fearful of what he might find. He winced as a couple of coughs escaped, making the searing line along his ribs flame up in pain again. More blood pulsed out. But he was pleased to see it was a gash in the flesh, but nothing more. He would need stitches, but his life wasn't immediately threatened.

There was a ripping sound, then Beckett said, "Here." He handed Crowley a wad of material torn form the bottom edge of his toga.

"Thanks." Crowley pressed it to his side, then accepted another strip from Beckett which he used to tie the first tightly in place. "That'll do for now," he said, doing his best to ignore the quite considerable pain.

Beckett helped him up, and Crowley looked down at Arundel's body.

"I still can't really believe it," Beckett said, hanging his head in shame.

"You never had any suspicions about Arundel?"

Beckett let out a rueful laugh. "Oh, I knew the man was a criminal. He stole, he cheated, he sold marijuana to children for goodness sake. But I never suspected he would be a murderer! Perhaps that makes me stupid. It feels like it now."

"Stole and cheated?" Crowley asked.

Beckett looked up, face sad. "Come on, I'll show you."

He led Crowley up out of the Sanctum and down a long stone hallway.

"Where is this place?" Crowley asked. "Above, I mean. Where are we?"

"It's a system of caves on Arundel's land. A lot of money and secret labor turned them into these stone passages and the Sanctum back there, and connected them up to the old Roman sewers under the village." Beckett cast a wistful glance back over his shoulder. "As boys, Arundel and I discovered the cave which is now the sanctum while exploring the grounds. At first we never told anyone. When Philip inherited the estate, he paid people to secretly start fitting the place out, villagers who were also part of the club, so we knew they wouldn't tell anyone. The vault, however, we did that ourselves. He and I and an awful lot of hard work to make sure it remained truly secret."

"The vault?" Crowley asked.

They turned a shallow bend in the passage and Crowley saw they'd reached an arched door, solid dark wood, banded in iron, with a heavy lock. The door was set in a stone wall that had itself been built into the passage, neatly fitting into the curves and crevices of the old cave. "The vault," Beckett said, gesturing at the door.

A gladius hispaniensis, or "Hispanic sword", hung on the wall right beside the arched wood. Crowley recognized the weapon as a mainstay of the Roman Legions. Beckett slid the gladius aside to reveal an entirely modern keypad.

Crowley leaned to the side to watch as Beckett tapped in a code. 5-8-6-4-2. Crowley committed the number to memory, just in case. The door clicked and opened an inch. Beckett pulled it wide and stepped back for Crowley to look in.

The vault was huge, at least thirty feet square. The rear and side walls were rough stone, the original cave. Adding the front wall and door must indeed have been hard labor, as Beckett had said. Inside the vault were hundreds of archaeological treasures. Artifacts from the era of Roman occupation, weapons and household items both, coins, jewels, jewelry.

Crowley was stunned. "This is an amazing collection. Is it all genuine?"

Beckett nodded. "Every bit."

Crowley frowned, looking at an old sword with a pitted blade. He picked it up to look more closely, saw several more nearby. "Are these from the battle of the Blood Field?"

Beckett deflated slightly and nodded again. "And therein lies the real secret. All of this was found in Wellisle."

Crowley turned, eyebrows high. "Seriously? That's what Arundel was killing to protect?"

"So it would seem. When Arundel and I were in our first year at the school, we stumbled across some Roman artifacts while on a history club outing. We'd unearthed an old pit, revealed from a slight landslip after some storms. We immediately suspected the things we found in there," he gestured to the sword in Crowley's hands, "those things, were artifacts from the battle. And we immediately realized that we were, in fact, in Wellisle. Close to the border between the two villages, certainly, but most definitely on the Wellisle side. Arundel demanded of me that we keep our find a secret and I agreed. It made perfect sense. I'd probably do it again. But I wouldn't kill to keep that secret! Several of the boys in the history club were from Wellisle. It was a mixed group then, before it became the exclusive Scarston club that you know today. Those boys would have never kept the find a secret, of course. Definitive proof that Wellisle was the battle site? So Arundel and I began making secret excursions back to the pit at night. We ferried everything to the safety of the caves we'd discovered on his father's estate. We started metal detecting in the area and made a wealth of findings. Incredible things, and all of them in Wellisle. Arundel insisted that we had to make sure no one ever found out, which meant we had to excavate the artifacts ourselves, always careful to conceal our work.

"But in the end, we had to admit that we needed help, so Arundel enlisted the help of a handful of boys from the oldest remaining Market Scarston families. We declared that we were no longer interested in the old history club, and were forming a club of our own, only for Market Scarston boys."

"And Ludus Historia was born," Crowley said.

Beckett smiled sadly, nodded. "Arundel had always been obsessed with all things Roman, including the mystery cults. Especially Mithraism. He seized the opportunity to create his own Roman cult, styled after the largely unknown Tauro Solis."

"And you went along with it?" Crowley said.

"We were thirteen-year-old boys. A secret society, training as gladiators? We thought it was great fun. And Arundel was a charmer, charismatic. He's always been a born leader of men; people just do what he says. It's a rare skill he has." Beckett's face paled slightly. "Well, had. We were all only too happy to go along with it. And besides, we were doing it for Market Scarston, weren't we? To preserve the only thing we had left to take pride in. To preserve our place in history."

"But that history is a lie."

For a moment Beckett looked at Crowley with something like pity. "History has always been the opinion of the victor. Never the truth."

"Is this everything you've found?" Crowley asked.

Beckett shook his head. "There was more. We've sold a lot of items on the black market over the years, always anonymously, of course. Mostly old coins and gems. It's helped to keep the school running. At least, it did. I suppose I'll have to notify the police, tell them everything. This might be the end of the school."

Crowley frowned. "Surely not. Arundel was the killer, but is any of this illegal? You've been lying about the history, but is storing this stuff away really a crime?" He genuinely had no idea what the answer to that was, but privately he couldn't imagine what might happen next.

Beckett looked around at the treasures. "If nothing else, I suppose the truth will finally come out. This will be a terrible blow to Market Scarston." He picked up a statue, turned it over in his hands. Then he looked up, his eyes haunted. "Will you give me a minute, before we head back up?"

Crowley nodded. "Sure."

As sick as the whole thing was, he understood why these treasures were so special to Beckett. He tried to imagine the boyhood excitement of their finds, the thrill of the secret caves and the secret club. It could have all gone on harmlessly and indefinitely if Arundel hadn't been such a lunatic. If he hadn't truly believed the mystery cult superstitions.

As he left the vault, hand pressed to his wounded side, he heard voices. He followed the sounds, back to the Sanctum, and saw Tommy and Morgan standing beside Philip Arundel's corpse. The sword still stood up from the man's chest, blood soaking the stones of the terrace beneath.

"You shouldn't have come back," Crowley said.

They both startled, looked up. "We got halfway back to the village," Morgan said. "Then Tommy changed his mind, determined to have it out with his father. He ran back and I chased him."

"You killed him?" Tommy asked, looking up at Crowley. He didn't seem sad or angry, simply resigned.

"No. We fought, and he would probably have killed me if it wasn't for Beckett. He killed your father."

Tommy's eyebrows rose in surprise. "I never would have believed he had that in him. I'll have to thank him."

"He's in the treasure vault," Crowley said. "Come on. Let's go and get him and get out of here. I think we need to call the police. And not the local police."

They went back along the hallway to the vault and Morgan's hand shot up to her mouth, as if trying to hold in the gasp that escaped. Crowley and Tommy just stared.

Beckett lay still on the floor among his treasures, blood pooling from where he had thrown himself onto one of the Roman swords.

29

Scarsdell Academy

Crowley sat across the desk from Elizabeth Morgan in the Headmaster's office of Scarsdell Academy. His side still hurt, the stitches itched as it healed, but after a week it was finally starting to come good.

"I'm as surprised as you," Morgan said. "But I'm only acting head. For the time being."

Crowley laughed. "Other than me you're the newest one here."

"I know! But none of the other teachers wanted the responsibility, so they said. What they mean is they don't want to be handed a cursed chalice. But I'm local, and that carries weight around here, even if you aren't one of the *better* class." She sighed. "And, I can't bear to see the school go under. So, I'll take it on. We're fully co-ed now, we're in a position to make good, positive changes, and we can have the school support itself without secrets and black market antiquities trading. I hope."

"Well, good for you."

"But I can't do it without help."

Crowley smiled. "The other teachers are staying."

"Almost all of them, yes. I managed to convince them to stay on. But I need you too."

Crowley leaned back and sighed. "I'll be honest with you, I've learned a lot about myself recently. I come from a certain privilege, I won't lie about that. But it's not who I am, not really. I would like to work in the public school system, in the city somewhere. I want to help kids who don't have all the advantages that Scarsdell kids are born with."

"I respect that, but I really need your help right now."

"Do you?" Crowley sat forward again, trying not to wince as his stitches pulled. "Could I remind you that not long ago you were asking the staff what was the point of me. Not even the point of me teaching here. 'What's the point of him?' you demanded in that staff meeting. Then, when Tommy first went missing, you said 'I don't see what you need him for.'"

Morgan's cheeks colored slightly, but she gave an impish smile. That smile was full of cheek and a kind of promise. Crowley liked it. "I didn't like you," she said. "But I'm big enough to admit I was wrong about you. And I need your help."

"So, you like me now?"

They stared at each other, Morgan's smile still in place. The air between them seemed to sizzle slightly. Crowley said, "Perhaps I could be convinced to stay for just a little while, if it wasn't all about work."

"We could *perhaps* find something to do outside of work hours too," Morgan said.

Crowley sat back again, more than a little pleased with himself. "Why don't I stay until at least the end of the school year then? When school breaks up next summer, I'll reassess."

"Thank you, Jake. I really appreciate that."

"You're welcome, Elizabeth."

She smiled. "You know what? You can call me Beth."

"This must remain a secret and exclusive in terms of numbers," Chas said.

The handful of teenagers in the history club room nodded. Emma put her hand on Chas's knee and gave him an encouraging nod.

"Tommy?" Chas said.

"Yeah?" Tommy was uncertain, but he wanted to be

with his friends. Nats sat beside him, Bradley Davenport on the other side. He felt suddenly self-conscious, singled out.

"I'm not proposing I do this alone. The leadership needs to be shared. And shared equally. Will you run it with me?"

"I don't know, man."

"Come on," Chas cajoled. "You're born for this."

Others in the room added their voices in encouragement.

"There are thirteen of us here," Chas said. "This is it. The whole group. This is what it'll always be, with you and me looking after things. What do you say? There's too much history to simply let it all go. We just do it right now, that's all."

Tommy took a deep breath, then blew it out again. It was appealing, the idea of being in charge of something, no longer under his father's awful shadow. "Okay then!"

The room erupted in cheers. Chas patted the air until they quieted again. "Ludus Historia is dead and gone," he said, his tone grave. "Long live Historia Scarstonia!"

The End

ABOUT THE AUTHORS

David Wood is the USA Today bestselling author of the popular action-adventure series, The Dane Maddock Adventures, and many other works. Under his David Debord pen name he is the author of the Absent Gods fantasy series. David and his family live in Santa Fe, New Mexico. Visit him online at www.davidwoodweb.com.

Alan Baxter is a British-Australian author who writes supernatural thrillers and urban horror liberally mixed up with crime and noir, rides a motorcycle and loves his dog. He also teaches Kung Fu. He lives among dairy paddocks on the beautiful south coast of NSW, Australia, with his wife, son, dog and cat. Read extracts from his novels, a novella and short stories at his website – https://www.warriorscribe.com– or find him on Twitter @AlanBaxter and Facebook, and feel free to tell him what you think. About anything.

CPSIA information can be obtained
at www.ICGtesting.com
Printed in the USA
BVHW030919160520
579798BV00001B/340